When she lands her dream job, Maya Scott thinks her luck may finally be about to change. Eager to prove herself a successful adult and win back custody of her young daughter, Maya is determined to excel at the Mars Fund. Her new boss, New York's notorious ice queen, Elena Mars, could prove difficult to please. Their relationship gets off to a rocky start and Maya learns from her coworkers, some who love her while others loathe her, that Elena has Cerebral palsy.

Embarrassed by her assumptions, Maya avoids Elena until the appearance of her Elena's young daughter at the office opens a line of communication and provides some common ground. A tentative connection blossoms between them and Maya realizes there is much more to Elena than the outward appearance. Between the complexities of learning about disability and navigating the distance between them in age and wealth, they find that what matters in the end is the family we choose.

D1744189

OFF BALANCE

L.E. Royal

A NineStar Press Publication

www.ninestarpress.com

Off Balance

Printed in the USA

Print ISBN: 978-1-64890-052-5

First Edition, August, 2020

Also available in eBook, ISBN: 978-1-64890-051-8

WARNING:
This book contains sexually explicit material, which is only suitable for mature readers, ableism, sexual assault (on page), mugging, workplace harassment, and homophobic slurs.

Chapter One

Hot coffee soaked the sleeve of her shirt. The elevator was packed tight as they ascended the staggering height of the office building. The shining chrome of The Mars Fund sign greeted Maya. She stumbled into the lobby, finally catching her breath and then losing it again when she looked at the opulent marble clock on the wall. She was late.

Blonde hair billowing out behind her, she burst into the office space, cheeks beginning to flame as all the eyes in the room turned to her and her urgent entrance.

"Maya, you made it!" Margaret, the overly friendly lady with the pixie cut and cardigan who had interviewed her for the position, called to her.

"I am so sorry. The bus was late and there was a huge line for the elevator."

Margaret was already waving off her explanation as she led her over to the desk she had inhabited the previous day, today being her second as a project coordinator at the Mars Fund.

"We're all still working on the preliminaries for the winter benefit," Margaret explained.

Maya nodded as she hurriedly stripped out of her leather jacket, grateful as ever for the relaxed dress code. She plopped down into her swivel chair, tight jeans and a thin black T-shirt clinging to her body. She rushed to turn on her computer.

"Miss Mars is back at work today."

Maya looked up. She studied Margaret as she offered her a noticeably tentative smile with the words.

"It's probably best if you just stay out of her way while you're getting the hang of things. I imagine she'll be busy in her office all day, anyway, catching up from yesterday."

With a pat on her shoulder Margaret was gone before she could reply, and finally, she was free to take a breath and let some of the stress from her hectic journey to work leave her. She *needed* this job; she could not afford to mess up.

Once she'd logged into her computer, she went back to the list of attendees she'd received and continued to work on emailing each of them to inform them of the benefit event the Mars Fund was planning for late in the year.

"Glad to see you made it, love." A male voice interrupted her, and she threw a quick smile to Kevin, her neighbor to the left, who seemed to be reclining in his chair doing very minimal work as he had done most of the day before. "Better watch yourself now, Scott. The evil old boss lady is back, and she'll eat a pretty little thing like you all up, given half a chance."

At first, she had been glad for Kevin, a seemingly instant friend, but as yesterday had worn on, and he leaned over toward her again, he was starting to irk her.

"Looks like you're going to be on her hit list, too, if you don't get back to work," she told him.

Seeming to take the hint, he tipped his head in silent concurrence and turned back to his own screen.

Getting lost in a blur of names and emails, she tried not to think too much about her boss. The woman was a bitch—that was the impression she'd received from the moment she stepped foot in the building. In her interview Margaret had been sweet, a little nosy but warm and welcoming, yet even she had clammed up when talking about the elusive *Miss Mars.*

The mood yesterday was jovial. Kathryn had perched on the edge of her desk for a good half an hour, and Maya was surprised to find she liked her as well as Dave and Graham, who had both welcomed her to TMF too. Today, the atmosphere was positively somber in comparison. The office was silent save for Kathryn talking softly into her phone and the click of keyboards. The presence of their boss hovering ominously over them all was palpable.

Another hour bled away, and she was pleased with the progress she was making on her list. Clicking out of her email program and back to her spreadsheet, she scanned down until she reached the next name. Robert Holt. Her blood turned to ice in her veins, and without thinking, she closed the window and shot up out of her seat. Heading for the restroom, she tried unsuccessfully to steady her ragged breathing.

She burst through the door, let it swing closed behind her, and leaned back against the cool wood, shutting her eyes. Her heart was hammering, a frantic staccato she fought to get under control. *I can't let him ruin this for me, again.*

The shock of seeing that name, of having it touch even this, taint it so soon, sent panic spilling through her, choking her and making it hard to breathe.

She opened her eyes at the sound of a toilet flushing and watched a woman step out of the stall. Jarred completely from her panic by the surprise of not being alone, her mood dissolved into a shy sort of embarrassment because this woman was gorgeous.

The stranger's dark eyes nailed her to the door, and even glaring daggers in her direction, Maya couldn't help but think she was beautiful and probably ten years older than herself. Thick mahogany hair hung down to her shoulders; she had smooth caramel skin and dark expressive eyes. A beat passed between them, too fast and too slow, and Maya pushed off the door, meaning to introduce herself. When the woman moved forward, her shoulders rocked back and forth, her hands clenched and jumped by her sides, and oddly enough she looked like she was dancing.

"I—um, having a good day?"

Not her greatest entrance, she could admit.

The woman's stoic expression was completely at odds with the jovial movement of her body, and Maya smiled tentatively at her, wondering if perhaps she was drunk or high.

She gripped the porcelain of the sink with tan fingers and seemed to steady herself some. As she turned to fully face Maya her head bobbed slightly, sending her hair dancing around her face. She was undeniably beautiful and odd.

"Do I look like I'm having a wonderful day?"

The words were pure venom, dripping disdain, a dark fire blazing in her eyes, and all the levity left the room. Maya's brain grappled to put together the pieces: the slight tremor in her frame, the occasional rock of her hips, and the way her fingers bounced lightly on the edge of the sink.

"Are you drunk?" And apparently today her brain to mouth filter was completely broken. *Crap.*

The woman advanced on her at an alarming pace, stiletto heels ringing out her steps, one, two, three, until

Maya was back against the door and staring down one hundred and twenty pounds of furious Latina in a business suit.

"Do you need help?" She tried again weakly, still not grasping what was happening, still reeling from the name on the list and the turbulence of this rapidly spiraling encounter.

"What I need is for you to tell me who the hell you are?"

Maya swallowed thickly. The woman was close enough that her breath was soft on her cheek, and she definitely didn't smell like she just came from the bar. Her perfume was light, pleasant, and smelled expensive.

"My name is Maya Scott. I'm a project coordinator for the Mars Fund... I—um, who are you?"

The woman sneered, and God, anything that terrifying should not also be that sexy. Her head still rocked every so often, her shoulders jumping occasionally, something slightly off in the way she spoke. Her eyes darkened as if irritated by her own movements.

"Elena Mars. I do believe I'm your boss, Miss Scott."

Her stomach dropped into her shoes, and Maya wondered momentarily if she was about to pitch forward and puke all over Elena Mars's expensive black patent Louboutins. She could not lose this job, and things were off to a less than wonderful start if this woman was her boss.

"I'm sorry, ma'am. I just—"

"Enough," Elena snapped, silencing her.

Maya had never felt more underdressed, her messy blonde curls hanging over her shoulders and her plain black shirt wilting next to Elena's perfectly tailored, crisp dress-and-blazer ensemble.

"I do not care who put you up to this." The final word was slurred slightly as Elena's mouth seemed to jerk sideways against her will. Even beneath her tan complexion, her cheeks colored slightly in response, and her eyes turned steely. "While you're in my employ, you will respect me. Is that clear?"

The words had something oddly toneless to them, and she rocked on the spot as she spoke. Maya nodded frantically, desperate to apologize, to somehow find a way to explain.

"Return to your desk and have Margaret show you the employee bathroom. This one is mine, exclusively."

"I'm so sorry. I just—"

"Leave." Elena took one shaky step back, teetering on her heels so badly that Maya almost reached out to steady her. Thinking better of it, she turned and quickly yanked open the door. She rushed back out into the hallway and headed for the office, her cheeks burning, dread clawing at her throat.

She needed this job.

"So, you met the evil bitch then?" Kevin's eyes were back on her before she had even sat down at her desk. "We did try to warn you, but you ran out of here so fast I suppose you didn't hear. Too much coffee?"

She offered him a weak smile and then scrubbed her eyes with the heels of her hands, attempting to shake off the mortification shrouding her. Her heartbeat was loud in her ears, and she was busy trying to breathe, to breathe around and through and over Robert Holt and Elena Mars and all the ways she might have ruined this for herself before it could really even start.

"Don't worry about it, love. She gets her kicks making us feel like shit. She's probably in her office downing half a bottle of whiskey and watching those Spanish sitcoms while we're all out here running the gig. Everyone knows she only has the job because Mommy owns the foundation."

Maya opened her mouth, trying to assimilate the information into her already clamoring brain while formulating a way to politely ask what the hell the nationality of the sitcom had to do with anything when Margaret appeared.

"Kevin, that's not true and you know it. Elena can be...difficult, but she works really hard for the foundation."

"When she's wasted." He muttered the words under his breath, causing Margaret to tut and perch on Maya's desk, blocking him from her view.

"Maya, Elena has a...medical problem, cerebral palsy. That's why she sometimes makes strange gestures and odd movements and can't seem to sit still. She's not drunk, so please don't listen to Kevin."

Maya's heart plummeted into her stomach, and she felt like such a fool.

"She is strict, and she can be difficult to work for, but I've worked with her for four years and known her much longer, and some of the events she's pulled off and all the money she has raised, it's amazing," Margaret continued. "She's helped an awful lot of kids."

Pieces fell into place with a horrible click. No wonder Elena had been so defensive and seemed embarrassed, though Maya had no way of knowing she had a disability. She wished silently that Elena would simply have explained it, rather than reacting like she had, though her own ignorance and lack of thought before she spoke bothered her the most.

"I had no idea..."

Margaret patted her shoulder kindly.

"She's very abrupt and can come off a little stern." A scoff from Kevin punctuated the statement, and Margaret paused to glare over her shoulder at him before she turned back and offered Maya a reassuring smile. "Elena values people who work hard and add something to the foundation. Just continue to do your best and I'm sure you'll have nothing to worry about."

Even as her supervisor walked away, Maya struggled to find comfort in the words.

She reached behind her into her jacket pocket to pull out her phone. She hit the home button and lit up her lock screen. A little girl with long blonde curls and emerald-green eyes like her own smiled back at her.

She could do this. She needed this job, and she was not going to let Elena Mars take it from her.

*

Three weeks later, Maya was finally starting to see a future for herself at TMF. Her emails had received many replies from wealthy supporters and attendees for the event, and Margaret had been pleased. The winter benefit was an amazing affair, gathering all of New York's who's who, as well as important figures from across the country, for a night designed to raise funds for children's charities that really needed them. Maya still couldn't quite believe she had a part in it.

The city was dark outside the office window. When she finally looked up from the procurement list she had been working on, the sun was long dead below the horizon, and she was alone. Saving her work and logging out of her computer, she wondered if there was a protocol for being the last person to leave the floor—Margaret had never mentioned anything as far as she could remember. Though she had stayed late every night this week, she'd never been there after Margaret had already left too.

"Miss Scott."

The smoky voice she had come to dread summoned her, and *of course* Elena was still here. Dutifully she stood and made her way down the hall to the place she had come to fear.

"Yes, ma'am?" She leaned around the door to Elena's office, letting out a quiet exhale and hoping the interaction wouldn't last too long. Since "the bathroom incident," as she'd taken to calling it in her head, she'd run into her boss very little, and aside from a few emails and one commendation on her performance received through Margaret, they hadn't spoken at all.

Elena was leaning back in her chair, each hand resting on an arm, perfectly manicured red nails stark against the black leather upholstery.

"Miss Mars is fine, or just Elena." An amused smirk tugged at her full lips, painted a softer red to match her nail polish that day. She was beautiful as ever, but in the dim light of her office, reclined in her chair, she looked smaller, tired. Maya noted that her hands only trembled slightly against the armrests, and her posture was as perfect as it always seemed to be when she walked through the office with only the occasional jolt tipping her slightly sideways.

"I've noticed you've been working hard; thank you."

Though it was true, somehow it was the last thing she had expected Elena to say. Emboldened by the praise, she stepped fully into the doorway and hovered there.

"Thank you, I'm enjoying the work, and it's amazing to know we're making a difference, you know?"

Elena simply nodded, though she was studying her with an intensity that made the hairs on the back of Maya's neck rise and her stomach do strange things. The silence stretched on. Maya allowed herself to drink Elena in as her dark eyes roamed further down her legs, and she noted Elena seemed to have no issues doing the same.

She was gorgeous, full figured, and oozing sensuality. She was powerful and successful and desirable in a way Maya knew she would never be. If they had met in one of the bars she sometimes frequented in the gay district, she could imagine their interactions being very different and entirely more pleasurable. The thought made her mouth water. She ran her tongue over dry lips before she swallowed and let that train of thought slip away as Elena spoke.

"I suppose you should be going then. I'm sure you have plenty to get home to."

She wasn't sure if the assumption was meant as a dismissal or a way to continue the conversation. She answered anyway, eager to stay bathed in the soft glow of Elena's office, to remain under the gaze of her dark-coffee eyes for a while longer, rather than rushing home to be alone in her apartment.

"Actually no, not tonight, anyway..."

Elena didn't seem offended by her rambling. She jerked slightly in her chair, her fingers tapping against the armrest before she brought her hands into her lap, clenching them into a fist to quell the movement.

"How about you? You've been here when I left every night this week, you must be exhausted?"

Elena laughed, the sound bitter and mocking; though as her gaze dropped to linger on the smooth mahogany of her desk, Maya realized the sound was not meant for her.

"Exhausted, yes." The air was thick with something, and Maya got the impression that she wanted to say more. For a moment she thought she would, but when she returned her eyes to Maya's, they were cool again, and she could sense the moment was lost.

"Goodnight, Miss Scott. Thank you for your hard work this week."

The dismissal stung, left her lonely in a way she couldn't name. She moved from her place in the doorway, looking back over her shoulder as she pulled her leather jacket tighter around her to prepare for the cold February night.

"Goodnight, Elena."

Chapter Two

It was Friday, and Maya yearned for the weekend. Though the job she'd initially found so hard to believe she deserved was consuming her more every day, it was hard work. As she learned the ropes, she steadily gained more responsibilities. Margaret granted her the lead on overseeing the designers and furnishing rentals for the décor for the winter benefit—an allowance she was half sure had come from Elena herself after their short conversation the previous night.

Her hair fell over her shoulder as she stood at her desk, head bowed, going over the floor plan one more time, making a few adjustments to allow for some of the entertainment she knew would be happening.

Kevin's quiet snickering beside her made her look up. She followed his gaze to the long glass wall that separated their communal office space from the kitchen and the employee restrooms. Looking back at her was Elena, her hands jerking erratically at her sides, her hips twitching every so often. They locked eyes across the space, and Maya ached down to her bones for reasons she didn't know. Those dark eyes somehow reflected back the loneliness she knew so well, and for a brief moment in time she ached to know more about the abrasive enigma that was Elena Mars.

"Earth to Scott."

Kevin was still laughing as he interrupted, but rather than acknowledge him, she watched Elena snap her eyes to him through the glass, her expression darkening before she turned away. Maya was already done with Kevin, all his pointed jibes and cruel jokes saying more about his personality than she was sure he thought his admittedly good looks did.

"Mama!"

Her favorite sound in the world cut into her thoughts, shattering the relative quiet in the room. A little voice she had not expected to hear until 6:00 this evening was summoning her excitedly from the doorway.

"Mama, Mama!" Livvie was calling for her, waving her little hand, desperate to be noticed, her long blonde hair in two neat braids that Maya's own fingers would never be nimble enough to make. Holding on to the hood of Livvie's winter coat, stony-faced and waiting for her, was Robert Holt.

Her heart hammered in her chest as she rushed across the space, her plans forgotten. She crouched down to meet Livvie, who was waiting to wrap her arms around her neck.

"Hi Livvie Bug, hi." Pulling her little daughter back, she looked her over, inspecting her for harm or any other explanation as to what they were doing here at her workplace in the middle of the day—not that she wasn't absolutely ecstatic to see her.

She pressed a quick kiss onto a cheek still cold from the lingering winter air, swung Livvie up onto her hip, groaning a little under her three-year-old weight, and faced the man who had brought her.

"Grandpa says we's starting weekend early!" Livvie crowed gleefully, and Maya bounced her lightly, more out of habit than necessity now she was bigger.

"Robert?" It was a greeting and a question, and Robert Holt smiled back his politician's smile, leaving her with no doubt this had been intentional.

"Good to see you, Maya. I sent you a text message last week. Bella and I are going out of town, and we agreed you would be taking Olivia a little early this weekend?"

Anger made everything in her chest feel hot, but somehow, holding on to Livvie, it was an easier pill to swallow. She fought the urge to correct him—her daughter's name was not and had never been Olivia. She should know; she had been the one to bring all seven screaming pounds of her into the world and spell it out for the birth certificate.

"Robert, I didn't receive any text message, and I'm working today."

He glanced around her, some of his usual condescension lacking from his gaze as he surveyed the office space.

"Yes, I see that. Looks like you're doing well for yourself."

He let the words hang, and in that moment, she hated him with the fire of a thousand suns, his motivation for all this finally coming clear—he was hoping to get her fired, again. She wanted desperately to say something, but past experience had taught her this was a fight she wouldn't win, and as inconvenient as it was, she was loath to send Livvie back to him after two long weeks of waiting to see her again.

"Did you bring a bag, Bug?" She turned her eyes to Livvie's, fighting to keep her cool. Bella, Robert's current wife and almost the same age as Maya, making her thirty years his junior, stepped forward with a small backpack.

"Everything she needs should be in here." Her smile was apologetic, and Maya almost, almost, could like Bella. She fixed Livvie's hair in so many beautiful styles, played with her, and read to her—Bella clearly adored her, but what she saw in a monster like Holt, Maya would never know.

"Thanks, Bella." She forced the words out, gaze falling almost of its own volition to Bella's prominent baby bump. Soon Livvie would be being raised alongside her aunt or uncle, and bitterly, she wondered why Holt still needed to keep her child when he would have his own.

"Well, if that's all, we'll be seeing you Sunday evening then." Holt stepped back, glee in his eyes as he patted Livvie on the cheek. Bella rushed forward and wrapped her arms around Livvie, bringing herself uncomfortably into Maya's space for a few too-long moments.

"Be good, sweetheart." She left a soft kiss on Livvie's cheek, and Maya was reminded again how hard it was to hate Bella Finch despite her horrible taste in men. Then she and Robert were gone.

"Mama you work?" Livvie asked, and Maya nodded, turning around to let her daughter better survey the office. The smile Livvie always brought to her face fell away as the sight of her coworkers, gawking at them both, greeted her.

"Um, guys... This is Livvie."

Not knowing what else to do, she hurried back to her desk. She dropped Livvie in her chair and gave her a blank notepad and a pen to scribble with before she rushed over to Margaret.

"I am so sorry, Margaret. I'm supposed to get her at six. I have no idea what he was thinking."

Margaret seemed concerned, and it made Maya's heart sink. She was finally starting to feel good enough, like she belonged at TMF, like she could do this. Once again, Robert Holt was going to snatch it all away.

"Nothing like this has ever happened before. Elena won't be happy. I'm not sure what to do. Perhaps it would be best if you just—"

"Well, hello." Elena's voice cut Margaret off, and Maya turned, watching with horror as her boss strode toward her daughter. The smile on Elena's face was blinding. "Does the Mars Fund have a special visitor?"

Livvie preened under the attention, rising an entire inch in her chair and turning on her best smile, complete with dimples, enthralled with the grown-up giving her undivided attention.

"Yes. Visitor. Mama works." She nodded to Elena as she pushed herself up to stand on the padded seat. Maya had taken one rushed step forward, moving to catch her before she could fall, but Elena was already there, her perfectly manicured fingers wrapped around Livvie's tiny ones, holding her up. The jerking of Elena's forearms caused their hands to move, and Livvie shrieked in joy, wiggling her hips along with the dance.

Maya's heart was beating against the inside of her ribcage to the point it hurt, full to bursting with the joyful laughter her daughter was releasing after two weeks of missing her, buoyed by the huge, genuine smile on Elena's face, yet terrified for how this interaction was going to play out. She could sense the rest of the office watching the pair too.

A long minute passed, and finally, Livvie plopped back into the seat with a thump, releasing Elena's hands in the process.

"Why you still dancing?" She beamed up at Elena, childish innocence in her eyes, as she watched Elena's body continue to move as she stood before her. Mortified, Maya rushed forward.

"I'm not dancing, I just like to keep moving." Elena was still smiling back down at Livvie as Maya rushed over, ready to chastise her for being rude. "My name is Elena. What's yours?"

"My name's Livvie Marie Scott," Livvie stated proudly. "You talk funny."

"Livvie!" Maya's cheeks burned, tears of mortification starting to prick the very backs of her eyes.

Elena's grip on her arm was firm and cool, even through her long sleeve, and Maya looked up to see the expression in her eyes was kind.

"That's quite all right, Miss Scott."

She turned back to Livvie, holding on to the edge of the desk as she leaned down closer to her.

"You're a very clever little girl, Livvie. I do talk funny because I have cerebral palsy. Have you heard of it?"

Livvie shook her head.

"Well, it means sometimes I move when I don't mean to, even my mouth, so you're right, sometimes I do talk funny as a result."

Maya watched, dread pooling in her stomach, as her daughter's intelligent green eyes zoomed in on Elena's face, suddenly fascinated.

"That why you dance?"

"I suppose so, yes."

The room was holding its breath, and Maya wished for the carpet to open and swallow her and Livvie and deposit them on the sidewalk outside the building and away from the absolute mortification she was feeling over her daughter's candid words.

"Can I have it too?" Livvie jerked her head and shoulders, rocking back and forth as she spoke, and Maya's mouth dropped open.

"Well, no, but perhaps I can tell you more about it. I have a new tea set I've been waiting for a special occasion to use, and some pages that really need coloring in my office. Why don't you ask your mama if it's okay if you attend a tea party this afternoon while she finishes up her work?"

Livvie scrambled down off the chair and stuck her hand out, finding her balance on her feet and looking expectantly at Elena. Maya's heart fluttered and melted as her boss reached out a shaking one to take it.

"Mama, me and Mm'lena have a tea party, 'kay?" Livvie barely looked back at her, besotted with Elena already, her other little hand stroking the satin material of Elena's dress skirt reverently.

"Elena, you don't have to—"

"Nonsense, Miss Scott, you are needed here, and we need those plans." Her tone left no room for disagreement, and Maya found herself nodding. "Can she have some apple juice and maybe something from the cafeteria—something nutritionally balanced, of course?"

Maya nodded dumbly, trying to muster the parental side of her to break through the surrealism of all this.

"Yeah...she doesn't have any food allergies or anything, so uh, she can eat."

Offering a tight but genuine smile to her and a subfreezing glare that sent the rest of the room scurrying back to work, Elena waltzed out, power suit, killer heels, and adoring three-year-old in her wake, leaving Maya to stare dumbly after her.

"Didn't know you were on first name terms with the bitch now, love."

She barely even heard Kevin's jibe.

*

The day passed too fast and too slow. Knowing Livvie was just a few walls away in Elena's office made it hard to concentrate. The two weeks at a time they were apart was always too long. As much as she couldn't wait to start her weekend with her daughter, she dreaded five o'clock, her stomach rolling uncomfortably every time she thought of facing Elena. She was sure she was going to be dismissed for this.

The office was oddly quiet since Livvie's impromptu arrival, and Maya could feel the judgments of her coworkers weighing on her like a physical touch.

At twenty-two, she was at least a few years younger than anyone in the office, and the surprise arrival of her daughter had incidentally outed her as a single mom, former teen mom, and a mom who had lost custody of her child all in one fell swoop. Even in her own head, the titles began to wound, picking away at the life she was building for herself here and leaving little scabs that bled and begged to be picked some more.

Forcing herself to focus, she continued to file her notes from the day, vendors lists and plans. Livvie was her proudest achievement. The circumstances around her birth and the current custody situation were less than ideal, but she had done the best she could through each of the defining moments that had been their life. She had to believe that, though some days it was easier than others.

Fortified by the thought, she pushed the papers into a neat stack, and glancing up at the clock—5:40—she decided it was time.

Nothing could have prepared her for the sight that greeted her through the open door of Elena's office.

"I am aware that it's only three days away."

Elena's gaze flicked to her as she hovered in the doorway, spellbound by the sight of Elena Mars, phone to ear, whisper-hissing as she chewed someone out mercilessly, with a very out of it Livvie fast asleep on her lap.

"That is not my problem..." she continued. "Yes, I'm absolutely fine, just fix it."

Maya stared and stared, unable to look away as Elena disconnected the call and set the phone down carefully on her desk. Her tan fingers smoothed back the blonde curls hanging over Livvie's cheek with an affection that was totally natural, and just as surprising.

"Miss Scott."

The greeting was soft, and Maya moved into the room, gesturing at the seat across from Elena, silently asking permission though her boss was preoccupied with adjusting the little head on her shoulder and didn't notice, so she sat anyway.

"Elena, I'm so sorry." She decided to start with her explanation, rather than sit there and wait for it all to come crashing down. "I wasn't supposed to have her today. Her grandfather just turned up here out of the blue. I know it's totally unprofessional, and I understand that we are probably so far behind it seems you had to spend all day babysitting my kid—"

"Miss Scott."

Elena tried to interrupt her, but she couldn't stop, unwilling to let her say the words and take away this job she had come to love, this stable future she was finally building against the odds.

"I can't tell you how sorry I am. I will work overtime next week or try to take some of it home. I can work next weekend, or whatever you—"

"Maya."

Her name was hissed, though not unkindly, the two of them talking in half whispers and hushed tones so as not to wake Livvie. It was enough to finally make her pause.

"While not ideal for business, today has been one of the best I've had for a while. Margaret stopped by before she left and informed me that the team accomplished everything we'd planned for the day and more."

She paused, her eyes suddenly elusive. Maya watched her in awe, and finally breathed because somehow, she didn't think she was getting fired. Not for the first time, she wondered how everyone else in the building genuinely believed this woman was an ice queen.

"Thank you for entrusting me with your daughter. We had a wonderful day. She's a very bright girl."

Elena gestured to her desk with the free hand that wasn't holding Livvie, and for the first time Maya looked down and noticed it was littered with drawings. Some scribbles, but some she could see Elena had drawn out the letters of her daughter's name in messy red dots and an unsteady hand had connected them with a fat marker.

"Wow...that...Elena, that's amazing."

She let her fingers reach up and trace the letters. Tears prickled, warm at the back of her eyes. Swallowing them away, she turned her gaze back to Elena.

"You're a natural... Do you have kids or—?"

Elena was glowing, but somehow, the question tainted that. A bitter scoff left her lips, and she turned her head away, though whether the movement was intentional or not, Maya couldn't say.

"No, no kids. I live alone."

Maya fumbled for the words while Elena smoothed Livvie's little fingers where they had balled into a fist around her blazer.

"CP isn't genetic."

It took Maya a moment to realize Elena was talking about her condition.

"No one put a curse on my mother's uterus. You can't catch it, and I wouldn't pass it on if I had a child... Though I'm almost thirty-seven and suspect the time for that has long since passed anyway."

She murmured the words, avoiding Maya's eyes, and Maya sat deathly still, silent, afraid to break this moment and to force Elena back behind the walls she seemed to exist inside most of the time.

"But who would want to have a child with me, like this?" The question was barely a whisper, and for the first time, Maya could see the longing in her eyes when she looked at Livvie. She wondered what the world had done to this beautiful woman to make her think she was somehow undesirable, undeserving of a family of her own.

The words she was trying to find, all the feelings, rushed forward, dancing in her chest and thick in her throat. She was searching for the right way to express them when Elena's eyes were on her again, hardened in a way that told her the conversation was over, though Elena still didn't seem as entirely closed off as usual.

"I enjoyed today. Thank you, Maya."

She nodded dumbly, choking on all the things she had wanted to say, frustrated that her moment to correct Elena, to tell her she was wrong, she was desirable, she was amazing and strong even underneath her harsh façade, and anyone would be lucky to have a family with her, had passed.

Chapter Three

"So, she just took the kid and took care of her all day, and that was that?" Winling's mug waved precariously as they spoke, earning them a dark glance from Livvie, before they quickly turned it right way up.

"Winling, no spill the tea!"

Livvie took a loud pretend sip and went back to carefully pouring imaginary tea into their mugs from the only good measuring jug in the kitchen.

Maya nodded, amused at her daughter's actions.

"Yeah. When I went to pick her up at the end of the day, I was sure I was getting fired, but she was fine about it, nice even."

Winling studied her with those dark eyes she knew saw far too much, though her best friend often said little. Maya was careful to avoid their gaze lest they read something in her own eyes that she wasn't ready to share or even acknowledge.

"Did you talk to Robert about showing up out of the blue?"

She shook her head, picking at a loose thread on her sweater.

"He and Bella are out of town this weekend. He didn't text me about it, Win. I even checked back through my phone. I'm telling you he's doing it again..."

A heavy silence hung between them, broken only by Livvie's soft humming as she continued with her tea party despite the adults, who were not even half playing at this point.

"You can't let him win, May. You're finally in a good place. If he starts trying to ruin it, you're going to have to call him on his sh...shiitake mushrooms."

Maya knew they were right, but the thought alone made her squirm. Robert Holt had held her under his thumb for so long—too long, three precious years of her daughter's life to be exact—and breaking out seemed almost impossible now, but she had to find a way.

"After he got me fired from the magazine, I promised myself I'm not doing this anymore."

Winling nodded emphatically.

"So, have you hired a family lawyer then?"

"Not exactly..."

Before Winling could go on another rampage about Maya getting a court date set, Livvie cut in again with a pointed jab at the empty mug in front of her.

"Mama, you tea is cold, and they's tea is cold."

Sufficiently chastised by her daughter, she obediently picked up her mug and took a long imaginary sip before setting it down, hoping Livvie would be satisfied.

"Please use a coaster, Mama. It good manners." She could practically hear Elena's voice in her daughter's, and the thought made her smile. Before she could think on it further, she grabbed her phone and snapped a picture of Livvie with her mug and jug-cum-teapot, not wanting to admit to herself just yet that she was playing with the idea of sending it to Elena.

"Mama, tell them to drink up... Mama says drink up." Livvie prattled to Winling, not really needing her input at all, and suddenly, Maya was proud of her little girl.

Explaining Winling's pronouns was something they had worried about after Livvie began to talk, but the need had never arisen. After hearing Maya using they/them and a few corrections, Livvie had settled right into it, ending Maya's nervous babbled explanation of nonbinary as not feeling like a boy or a girl with a very anticlimactic "okay, Mama." Watching Winling drink their pretend tea and make a request for another cup in an obnoxious faux-British accent, Maya was glad her best friend was in Livvie's life.

Their Sunday morning tea party and catch-up wore on uneventfully until Maya was leaning on the doorframe, seeing Winling out while Livvie lay on the sofa falling asleep to another one of her animated movies.

"So, what's she like then?"

Maya's heart stuttered because she already knew exactly who Winling was talking about. She didn't respond, just stared blankly as if she had no earthly idea.

"Elena. I mean week one you seemed pretty intimidated, and she sounded kinda like a bitch; now she's babysitting your kid and writing you a pass when the old asshole drops her on you in the middle of a workday."

"She's nice." Maya shrugged, uncomfortable but knowing she would have to give Winling more if she wanted them to drop it. "It was really cool of her to take Livvie like that, and she's really passionate about the work. She works harder than anyone else, so I think she's entitled to set a high standard because she leads with one, you know?"

Winling nodded, flicking their short-cropped hair back from their eyes, looking positively dapper in a very androgynous and flattering white button-up and jeans combo. Their Asian heritage gave them a slim figure, which Maya envied most days.

"Things are coming together for you, May, for real this time. You can do this; Holt can go f...fly a kite..." They glanced over Maya's shoulder, contenting themselves the almost-curse hadn't been heard by little ears, before they continued. "It's gonna work out."

Maya tried to let some of Winling's certainty leach into her bones as they pulled her in for a tight hug. She wanted it more than anything. After three years of waiting, and fighting, and being sabotaged by Holt, she wanted her daughter back—and her life.

When Winling disappeared into the elevator and the front door was closed, Livvie still being entertained by a singing snowman, Maya leaned against the cool wood. Without really knowing why, she pulled up the picture she had taken earlier, finding Elena's number that she had saved from the welcome package at TMF. Elena's dark eyes, heavy with sadness, the softness and the brokenness with which she had declared so certainly that nobody would want a family with her, haunted Maya and made up her mind.

Before she could think about it anymore, she pressed send, hoping the silly little snap would brighten Elena's day. With it done, she resolved to try to put Elena out of her mind, a feat that had been strangely difficult all weekend.

*

Another workday was winding down, and Maya found herself satisfied, a feeling that was growing increasingly familiar. Her work at TMF was important, and the fact she was helping kids and challenging herself made her days seem worthwhile in a way she had never known.

"I know it's early, but I'm already excited for this year's staff party. It's going to be a hoot with you here, Maya."

Kathryn was smiling at her. Only a few of them were left in the office, chatting and unwinding as they finished up their day.

"True, love. Sure you'll be the belle of the ball this year."

She ignored Kevin's smarmy remark, trying not to pay attention to the fact his comments about her looks were becoming more and more frequent.

"What party are we talking about?" She directed her question back to Kathryn, hoping Kevin would get the message and butt out of the conversation.

"Every year Elena's family throws us this amazing staff party as a sort of thank-you after she works our butts into the ground before the schools get out to raise loads of money for kids' summer programs and stuff... Anyway, it's amazing."

"Usually us and a few of the other floors get together in a nice hotel, good food, open bar, dancing." Kevin piped up to fill in.

Not being a social person, Maya wasn't as immediately excited as her coworkers. Though she did like Kathryn, and even Margaret was nice in her own way, she wasn't as thrilled at the prospect of a work event, though she supposed the chance to get to know her coworkers more could be fun.

"Can we bring a plus one?"

Kathryn nodded. "My husband Frank is coming. You guys will get along like a house on fire, I know it!"

Maya could feel Kevin's eyes on her, and she wasn't sure why until he spoke again, trying to sound disinterested.

"So, bringing a boyfriend? Wasn't sure if the little girl had a dad, being raised by the grandfather and all. Seems like an odd situation."

Her hackles rose at his prying, and not for the first time she wished he would disappear.

"No, just my best friend, and the rest of it really isn't your business, Kevin."

He held up his hands in mock surrender, and Maya ground her teeth, vying with herself to just let it die and hope he would do the same. Sensing the tension, Kathryn slipped into her coat and gave her desk one last cursory glance.

"Well, I have to hit the road. Hope everyone has a good evening. See you bright and early."

With that she was gone. Not wanting to be forced to spend more time talking to Kevin as they were the only two left in the office, Maya picked up a stack of invoices that needed Elena's signature and headed for her private office without giving herself too much time to think about it.

Elena never had replied to her message with the picture of Livvie, though the more she thought about it, perhaps it was for the best. Elena was her boss after all, and their relationship should probably stay professional, despite her impromptu stunt as Maya's babysitter. As much as she tried to tell herself it didn't, the lack of a response had stung and still did, but she was trying not to dwell.

When she knocked softly on the doorframe, Maya was greeted by Elena's tired eyes and a smile that didn't quite reach them.

"Miss Scott." Elena's body rocked in her chair, her head jerking sideways in a movement Maya knew now was not intentional. Dark circles hung heavy under her eyes, and somehow, today, she was just a little less put together, a little more undone than Maya had ever seen her before.

"Elena, how are you?"

She tried to remain professional, polite, wondering if her unanswered text message was hanging as obviously between them for Elena as it was for her.

"Fine, what do you need?"

Elena was curt, but not unkind, and Maya noticed the way her hands were gripping the edge of the desk, knuckles white from the effort. As she released one hand's vise grip to reach out and take the stack of papers Maya offered her, it shook badly.

A terse silence hung between them, and Maya floundered for a way to ask Elena if she was okay without offending her.

"Thank you for the photograph. It brightened what was otherwise quite a dull weekend."

Elena's voice was soft as she spoke, so soft that it caught her off guard, and Maya wondered if she had heard her correctly. Elena didn't pause from flicking through the shaking papers in her hands, signing messily here and there as needed without looking up.

"I um, thank you. Livvie had a great time with you; it's actually all she's talked about since."

Elena finally raised her head, a tired smile gracing her face, and Maya was struck again, caught off guard by just how beautiful her boss was.

"I see she took a liking to tea parties. I was surprised she'd never had one before."

"Not really my thing," Maya replied, slightly defensive on instinct.

"Of course, quite archaic these days, I suppose. Probably a little before your time."

"No." The ease with which she corrected Elena surprised her, but somehow, the divide Elena was building between them, the space, the pointing out of the age difference, or the class difference, or whatever other reason Elena thought Maya didn't know what a tea party was irked her.

"I've had a few tea parties in my time." She tried to let her tone lighten, playing with Elena's own words. "I just never really thought to have one with Livvie. I still see her as my little baby, you know? But what you did with her, the dots and writing her name, and giving her the responsibility with the tea party, she really enjoyed it, and I guess it showed me she's growing up."

Elena's expression turned apologetic, and Maya cut her off before she could begin.

"Don't apologize, please, it's great. We had a lot of fun with it this weekend, and I got in trouble for not using a coaster, multiple times."

The mirth in Elena's eyes bubbled over, and together, they shared a quiet laugh.

"I hope I didn't influence her too much." Elena was still smiling, and Maya shook her head.

"My three-year-old now has better tea party etiquette than me."

They both smiled at the sentiment, and it felt secret to Maya, precious in a way that she wasn't quite ready to name.

"Is everything okay, Elena? You seem..."

She was suddenly brave in the face of their camaraderie, though her courage failed her before the sentence was complete.

"Exhausted?" Elena supplied the word, the humor from their previous conversation leaving her eyes. "I suppose I am." A heavy sigh racked her slender, ever-moving frame. It sounded bone weary and Maya ached on her behalf. "I move, all the time, hardly ever stopping. Even though it's not productive movement, it doesn't achieve anything, it still tires me. All day, every day, my body is never still. That, combined with the focus it takes to overcome it and make productive movements, to get through the day, some days it's just—"

"Exhausting?" Maya dipped her head, trying to meet her dark eyes. Somehow this Elena, the one behind the mask, the woman she was catching glimpses of more and more, she was addicting.

"Yes, well, it's nothing I'm not used to."

She could see the walls resurrecting themselves, and the effort cost Elena, her hands white knuckled on the edge of the desk again in an attempt to remain still.

"Don't. Don't pretend like you're okay. It's amazing that you can do all this." Maya paused to gesture around. "I can barely get through my day sometimes and that's without the added strain of CP." She was proud of herself for remembering the abbreviation for Elena's affliction.

"Don't feel sorry for me, Miss Scott. I do not need, nor want, your pity."

"Good. Just because I can acknowledge you had a rough day doesn't mean I pity you one bit." Maya squared her shoulders, green eyes holding Elena's, a silent challenge, and a promise.

She had been there—teen mom, young woman in trouble with the law, unemployed and then fired, then unemployed again—and she knew the sympathy did absolutely nothing but rankle.

Elena's dark eyes burned back at her and she squared her shoulders.

"Do you want to share a cab home? I live... What?"

She didn't have time to consider where her offer had come from, or finish it, because once again, Elena was smirking at her.

"You think I can't drive?"

Maya knew her cheeks were coloring again, the memory of that first meeting in the bathroom coming back to haunt her, reminding her how much Elena hated to be underestimated.

"No need to be embarrassed, most people with CP can't. I'm fortunate."

When Maya didn't speak again, Elena's eyes hardened, and then she seized the moment.

"So, may I give you a ride home, Miss Scott?"

Maya heard her own voice already accepting the offer before her mind had really decided, something swirling in the pit of her stomach, something she would not name as excitement or nerves, or the slick swell of anticipation even though it felt eerily like it. Coworkers did this, right? Even if they were each other's boss, even if one was a notorious hard-ass and CEO of a huge amazing company like TMF? Maya stopped herself before she psyched herself out. It made no sense unless there was another reason for the offer.

"Livvie isn't home tonight, I mean...She's at her grandfather's."

"That makes no odds, Miss Scott. Do you need to gather your things before we leave?"

Elena was already moving, pushed up to an unsteady stand, before she seemed to find her balance and went about shrugging into her coat. Maya watched her for a second longer. Elena's slim tan fingers struggled with the buttons, and she had to force herself not to intervene, heading instead to collect her bag and jacket.

Returning to the main office, she noticed with annoyance that Kevin was still there.

"The eBay auction ends in two minutes. Didn't want to miss it." He offered as if by explanation, lest it actually look like he was working hard for once, God forbid. She nodded and gathered her coat and then shoved a stack of papers into her satchel, fighting the urge to check her reflection in her now dark computer screen.

"So, what are you up to tonight, Scott?"

She was opening her mouth to give him some vague nonanswer when a voice interrupted her.

"Maya, are you ready?"

Her name had never sounded so damned good, wrapped around teeth and tongue and drawled out in Elena's rough, smoky voice. When she turned to look at Elena, all the tiredness from earlier was gone, hidden from her frame, her eyes alight with a challenge, an intensity that made Maya's skin prickle.

"Oh, if you need a ride home, love, I'll take you. I'll be done in just fifty more seconds."

Kevin seemed oblivious to the tension in the room, and Maya couldn't even bring herself to turn and look at him with Elena's eyes smoldering on her own.

"Uh, that's all right, Kevin, Elena's taking me."

She was rewarded with a killer smile. Elena looked delighted and positively predatory, and it made her ache so hard she wondered if she was imagining all this because she was insanely attracted to her boss, since at this point it was undeniable that she was.

"Nonsense, Scott, I don't mind really..."

She turned to look at Kevin, about to lose her cool and tell him to mind his own business, but Elena was faster. She moved surprisingly quickly on three-inch heels with wickedly gyrating hips and shaking hands.

"Go home, Mister James."

Kevin's squeal of horror as he stared at his black screen was far from manly. His lips pulled back from shock to a sneer as he looked up to see Elena holding the plug for his computer between two perfectly manicured fingers.

"You fucking—"

"Me what?" She hissed the words back, her head jerking to the side erratically before she jerked it right back, daring him to continue.

He clenched his fists, and Maya stepped forward—to do what, she had no idea. Elena was electric in that moment, powerful and cool and razor-sharp, and for some reason Maya ached to run her fingers over her edges and let their bite consume her.

"Please refrain from using the office computers for your personal shopping, Kevin." Her voice was ice cold, but a challenge burned bright in her eyes.

Kevin said nothing, throwing his phone and charger roughly into his backpack and standing up to storm out. He paused by Maya, and she stepped back on instinct.

"Just so you know, Scott, she's a dyke."

Too stunned to respond, Maya stared dumbly at him until he left, her eyes then finding Elena whose cheeks were coloring visibly, even under her tan complexion.

A Hallelujah chorus was singing, and sirens were screaming, a joyful wail rolling around and around in her head—*Elena likes girls, Elena likes girls*—and she should not be as absolutely ecstatic at the revelation as she was.

"If you no longer want a ride, I understand."

Elena's voice brought her hurtling back to earth. Elena who had just been outed in the cruelest way, Elena who was swaying again, fingers tight around the edge of Kevin's desk, that tiredness back in her eyes.

Maya stared at her. "I do... I mean, I want one, if that's still okay?"

Elena nodded and turned to leave. Maya followed her wordlessly and waited behind her as she called the elevator. They descended to the parking garage, the silence between them suddenly stony. Taking a deep breath, she breeched it.

"I'm sorry he said that. It's a disgusting word used in that way, and I can't believe he has the nerve to speak to anyone, especially you, like that since you're his boss."

"Kevin's father and my mother are good friends. He knows his position here is secure no matter how he treats me."

The response was clipped and emotionless, and as Maya followed Elena toward a sleek black Mercedes, one of the last cars in the lot, anger made her blood too hot in her veins.

"That's not okay. He shouldn't be able to speak to you that way and keep his job. You shouldn't have to deal with that."

Elena unlocked her door without a word and slipped into her side of the car. Still incensed, Maya did the same.

Elena started the engine, and Maya watched with fascination as she operated the machine that was quite different to any traditional vehicle she had seen.

"Address?"

Elena didn't look at her as she punched a large button on her GPS, instead letting the mic pick up her voice as she rattled off her address. The drive continued in tense silence, broken only by the robotic voice giving verbal directions until, finally, Maya was brave enough to try again.

"Elena, what he said, I don't care. It wasn't his place to tell, but it doesn't matter, and it really doesn't change anything."

Elena was stiff in her seat, and Maya watched fascinated as she held her thumb on a button and the car sped faster.

"Thank you. It's always nice to have an ally."

She was doing it again, distancing them, creating space between them and making them separate, and Maya hated it.

"I'm not just an ally. Can't say I identify as a *dyke*, and I'm sure you don't either, but he insulted more than one of us back there with his homophobic bull crap."

Elena's dark eyes were on her, so intense that Maya was momentarily tempted to prompt her to turn them back to the road, yet she couldn't break the spell. When Elena finally looked away, Maya sucked in a breath, realizing she had been holding hers.

"I suppose you're wondering about the car?"

She agreed and let the topic change easily, though she couldn't help but feel a little closer to Elena, thanks to her own admission. She listened intently as Elena explained how her car was modified with special controls to be easier for her to operate.

"That's amazing, there's so much I don't know." Maya was genuinely enthused and amazed by the subject.

"If you mean about CP, I'm probably not the best example. I was very fortunate as a child. My parents didn't believe I should be treated any differently because of it.

My elder sister walked, so I was going to walk. If Zara was mopping, I was mopping."

The smile on her face was almost fond, and Maya caught herself smiling along with her.

"My father taught me to walk by standing my feet on his feet and then waving candy in front of me for me to chase after. That was when I was five."

They both shared a laugh.

"Always been a go-getter then?"

Elena just laughed a little harder.

"I went to public school and five years of speech therapy so I could live as much like a 'regular' person as possible. That was always my mother's goal. Most people with CP aren't able to walk. I am extremely lucky in that respect. I have my mobility."

The mood sobered, and Maya felt ignorant in the wake of how little she knew about this, about modified cars and years of speech therapy that made the hardships in her own life come into stark contrast against all the ways she was so very privileged.

"You're kind of amazing."

She hadn't meant to say the words out loud, to let them be so sincere and reverent, but as they idled at a stoplight and Elena smiled across at her, that beautiful, shy, genuine smile, she couldn't help but be glad she had.

Chapter Four

"You know it makes sense, May. Come on."

Winling was being persistent tonight, more so than usual, and although they had a valid point—several, actually—Maya just could not muster the excitement her best friend felt at the prospect of a night out on the town.

"Let me be old." She grumbled into the bowl of cereal that was her dinner.

"Maya, you're wearing fuzzy socks and a Beatles T-shirt and planning to spend your night holed up with a blanket and an unhealthy amount of hot chocolate, all alone...again."

"Exactly, I'm old."

They groaned.

"We should celebrate... I mean, Holt seems to have backed off. You're killing it at your awesome new job. Things are on the up. Who knows, maybe you'll meet someone?"

She swirled the spoon around in the bowl, knowing they were probably right. Things had been going well, and she kind of did need to get out more, maybe meet someone, do something outside of work and worrying about the custody situation with Livvie. There had been a time where the two of them would have nights out semiregularly, but lately, Maya found her interest had waned. A night in alone with a book or some bad TV just sounded so good to her, and for some reason, she didn't want to think about dating again right now.

"I'm just...not in a place where I want to meet someone. Life is good, so why complicate it? My sofa is comfy, so why leave it?"

Winling rolled their eyes. "Okay, crushes on bosses."

Guilt trickled into her chest at the words.

"What?"

"You totally have the hots for Elena. You should have heard yourself talking about that car ride, and newsflash, May, you talked about it *a lot.*"

They might be just a little bit right. She had told them about the night Elena had driven her home in great detail and spent a fair amount of time thinking about it too. She'd convinced herself it was because she was amazed by Elena as a person, definitely nothing more.

"I was just excited by the modifications on her car, and sure, I admire her. I mean the woman is a force of nature. I've seen her make a forty-year-old man cry like my kid when I say she can't order a twenty-piece nugget instead of a Happy Meal and cause an unholy meltdown."

Winling laughed; they both did. The brown eyes that knew her so well searched her face, and Maya knew they saw something there, something she wasn't ready to see herself perhaps, something she definitely didn't want to talk about. She caved.

"Fine. I'll go, but there's one condition."

Winling raised their hands in celebration.

"Name it, Scott!"

"The first round is on you."

*

Of course, they ended up in some hip new lesbian bar in the gay village that Maya had never been to before. They bumped into some of Winling's girlfriend Alicia's friends, Alicia herself currently out of the country in Milan or Paris or some equally amazing and obnoxious destination that Maya had definitely been told but didn't remember.

It was hilarious watching the brood of gorgeous ultrafemme women swoon over Winling in the absence of their girlfriend. She could tell they enjoyed the attention, but they kept from crossing any lines. It was obvious they, too, were fascinated by the back-stabbing rich girl world they had inadvertently become a part of when they began dating Alicia.

Maya nursed a beer, already tired of her Jack and Cokes and beginning to feel out of place. Winling had introduced her to the gaggle of girls, but beyond that, she had absolutely nothing to say and nothing in common with them. She sort of floated along, watching the conversation but not really joining in, which tended to happen on their nights out. Winling was a social butterfly; they could be stoic and leaned toward fewer words rather than more, especially around people outside of their immediate circle, yet somehow the limelight always seemed to find them.

She glanced around bored, and her heart stuttered as her eyes landed on the back of a brunette head. Straining to see through the thin throng of bodies in the low light, Maya leaned sideways in her seat, desperate for a better view, holding her breath. The woman turned, her gait and movements all wrong, and she knew it wasn't Elena. Her heart was still beating fast from the adrenaline that had surged into her bloodstream when she had thought her boss was there. She was still dissecting her own reaction when the woman she had mistaken for Elena noticed her staring and shot her a smile.

Maya smiled back on instinct.

She was older, not as classy as Elena, in tight jeans and a revealing halter-neck shirt that Maya could never see her boss wearing, but she was brunette, good-looking in a plain sort of way. When she approached, Maya didn't shrug her off.

She said her name was River, which sure, okay lady. She was thirty-five—two years younger than Elena, Maya noted mentally—and worked in the office at a mechanic shop.

"So, Maya." River's dark-blue eyes were on her, and after the three shots and another beer River bought for her, Maya was struggling to focus on her words. "I guess you like older women. It's either that or free drinks, right?"

Maya laughed more than was necessary. The laugh was nervous and pitchy, and her insides felt funny. Truth be told she had never been in a situation to consider older women, never really been interested in one until she met Elena. Not that she actually had a crush on her boss, but she was an adult; she could admit when someone was insanely attractive without being into them, of course.

"Age is just a number." She offered the words with a shrug, and that seemed to be enough for River. When she was dragged out onto the dance floor, she let herself go willingly, draining her glass and setting it on a table on her way.

It was cathartic for a while, moving to the music, feeling like she belonged as just another body inside the writhing entity of the whole crowd, but as River pressed closer, her buzz started to wane.

"Are you having fun, Maya?"

She closed her eyes and pretended it was Elena at her back, imagined the hands on her hips were tipped in that perfect crimson manicure, and the hair tickling her shoulder was a single shade darker of ebony-brown, and suddenly, she was.

She pushed back into Elena...River...and they danced two more songs, her liquor-riddled brain pushing her logical one back down a while longer, but when River's lips brushed her neck, reality finally won out.

"I really need to find my friend."

River looked betrayed, and Maya really hoped she didn't actually think she had used her for the drinks because she hadn't. If she was being totally honest with herself, she had entertained River longer than she usually would have because of her initial resemblance to Elena. The thought spilled a panicky feeling into her stomach, and with one last apologetic smile, she disappeared into the crowd, leaving River behind.

After two laps of the building and still no sign of Winling, she slipped out into the cold night and pulled out her phone to call them. It rang and rang with no response.

Leaning against the wall, she waited.

She worried about leaving them, but she also knew from experience that Winling had probably bumped into someone they knew and lost track of time and place. It happened. Not willing to give up quite yet, she decided to hang around a while longer to see if they came out for a smoke, a guilty pleasure of theirs they only indulged in while drinking.

Flicking through her phone, she absentmindedly scrolled down through her messages, pausing to hover over Elena's thread. When she gave in and tapped it, the picture of Livvie and her makeshift little tea set greeted her.

A scuffle broke out close by, surprising her. Still hazy from the liquor, she decided the best plan of action was to head home and call Winling when she got there to check in.

She walked for a while, hoping to run across a cab, her feet aching in her heels. When she still didn't find one, she yanked out her phone again, resigning herself to calling for one and waiting. Elena's name was on the screen. Confused, she lifted her cell to her ear.

"Elena?"

"Miss Scott!" Elena sounded exasperated.

"Did you call me? I—um...I'm not home."

When the reality that Elena was on the phone permeated her drunken state, she instantly panicked. Did she fuck up at work?

"No, you called me, quite a while ago I might add."

What was Elena talking about?

"No, I think you called me, there's no way I called you, I would remember. Oh, a cab!"

Maya waved frantically, flagging down the vehicle and climbing inside, forgetting momentarily about the call as she informed the driver of her address.

"...ya... Maya... Miss Scott?"

By the time she raised her phone back to her ear Elena was asking if she was still there.

"Yeah, I'm here. So why did you call me again?"

She leaned back on the seat letting the lights of the city lull her as they sped by, feeling a little tired and very tipsy.

Elena's huff was audible over the line.

"Where exactly are you?"

"I'm in a cab. Where exactly are you?"

"I'm at home."

Silence hung over them for a few moments, and Maya's eyes were beginning to drift closed when she was interrupted again.

"Are you alone?"

"Mmhmm."

"Miss Scott! It's awfully dangerous to be wandering around alone and riding in cabs by yourself at this time of the night!"

The chastising in Elena's tone jolted her awake.

"I'm fine but stay on the phone with me if you want to, and I'll let you know when I get home."

The line was silent for a beat.

"Fine."

The reply was terse, but tipsy-Maya didn't mind. They were quiet for another moment, and then, closing her eyes, she spoke again.

"So, what have you been doing tonight, Miss Mars?"

She used the title with enough emphasis to play with Elena, a smile on her lips.

"I went on a date."

The answer was as tight as the last, and Maya's heart fell. Probably due to the liquor and her own severely lacking love life, she told herself quickly. She definitely did not have a huge gigantic crush on her boss.

"How was it?"

That's what she'd ask Winling. Winling was her friend, and she and Elena could be friends, maybe?

"Honestly, it was abysmal. We spent half of it talking business and the other half figuring out that we want absolutely none of the same things."

"Sorry."

She didn't sound sorry, so Maya carried on quickly, eager to skirt over that minor detail.

"What do you want that she didn't?"

Elena was quiet for a long time, and Maya was drifting off again when she finally spoke, pulling her back.

"Walks in Central Park and days at the museum, nights in and home cooked meals...family."

She sounded sad. Maya thought that sounded wonderful.

"And what did she want?"

"Fancy restaurants and galas and six vacations a year plus lots of business trips."

"Ugh."

Elena laughed.

"Ugh indeed."

"Yours sounds way better, almost perfect actually, but you forgot one thing. Hot chocolate."

Maya glanced out of the window, guessing she was roughly ten minutes from home.

"Hot chocolate?"

"Yeah...with cream or marshmallows for the nights in."

"I don't usually like sweet but that—"

Elena stopped talking abruptly. Confused, Maya yanked the phone away from her ear and stabbed at the black screen. When she tried the lock button the empty battery icon greeted her, and she groaned.

Oh well.

In her still slightly drunk state, she didn't think too much of it. She could ask Elena what she was going to say about the hot chocolate on Monday.

Her head lolled back, and she closed her eyes, drifting, pleasantly lulled by the movement of the car until the cab driver banged on the glass between them and informed her that they had arrived.

Dutifully, she shoved her debit card into the slot and punched in her PIN, her finger annoyingly slipping off the numbers, so it took her two tries to get it right. She stabbed the button to give the guy a generous tip, grateful to have made it home, and thanked him again as she stumbled onto the curb.

The air was brisk, and it was well after midnight. She hurried as much as she was able for the door of her building, the world swaying slightly around her. Stopping to rummage in the pocket of her leather jacket, eager to find the keys and get out of the cold, she hovered by the building door.

"There you are."

The words were hissed from behind her and something touched her arm. She shrieked and whirled around, dropping her keys, and grabbed onto the person in fright.

"Oh my God... Elena?"

The adrenaline made her completely sober for a long five seconds. Then, as it left her chest and filtered out through the rest of her body, she felt even more drunk than she had been before. Clutching Elena's arm, she wondered if this was some wicked fantasy fulfillment hallucination or if her boss was stalking her. Was it stalking if you wanted to be stalked? She would have to ask Winling about that one.

"So, traipsing around the city at gone midnight and getting into a cab with who knows who is not a big deal for you, but I show up and now you're scared?"

"Oh shit, you're mad."

Elena rolled her eyes and bent with some difficulty. She scrabbled around a little before she used the door to pull herself back upright onto her feet. Nudging Maya out of the way, she struggled to fit the key into the lock with shaking hands.

"Not mad, I was worried. After all, the Mars Fund needs you. You're the best associate we've hired in years. I couldn't have you going missing, could I?"

"You came to check on me?"

Maya followed her inside, letting the hand around her arm tug her along toward the elevator.

"What floor?"

She looked down at the floor under her feet stupidly, her brain still trying to wrangle its way around the fact that Elena Mars was there with her in her building. *Holy shit.*

"Miss Scott, what floor do you live on?"

"Three."

She held Elena's gaze, studying her face, free of makeup and as beautiful as she had ever seen it. A thick wool peacoat hugged her body, black yoga pants poking out from beneath it and ending in soft suede boots. She was gorgeous, as always.

"Thank you." Elena's smile was soft and bashful and *oh God...*

Maya licked her lips and closed her mouth, silently trying to convince herself it was fine she had said that out loud... *Friends compliment each other all the time... Right?*

They stumbled out onto the third floor, both off balance for different reasons, and Maya marveled at Elena's surprisingly firm grip on her arm.

"Number?"

Already able to see her front door, Maya just gestured, and they set off again. Elena even went as far as unlocking that door for her, too, pushing her keys back into her hand and guiding her over the threshold.

"Goodnight, Miss Scott."

She gestured for her to head inside, but Maya's brain mercifully caught up or at least started to.

"Wait, how will you get home?"

She was painfully aware that Elena was leaving, and she didn't want their time together to end.

"I drove over, so I'll drive back."

"But where's your car? I should walk you to it."

She moved to step back out into the corridor when a firm hand on her shoulder stopped her.

"Go to bed, Maya. Drink a few glasses of water before you do. I'll be fine."

Even under the harsh fluorescent lighting she was beautiful, and Maya became aware she had been staring at her too long when, with another half smile, Elena turned unsteadily and began to head back toward the elevator.

"Elena... I'm sorry your date was terrible, or abysmal, or whatever you said..."

Elena paused, their eyes met, and in that moment, Maya ached to know her.

"Me too."

She wasn't sure if Elena had shrugged or just jerked. She watched her reach up to hit the elevator call button, missing it once before she was able to punch it. She wanted to call her back, stop her, invite her inside.

"Elena..."

She turned.

"I... Do you... Um..."

Even with the liquor still potent in her bloodstream, it took a little more courage than she had available to invite her in. Elena's eyes were on her, expectant, maybe even a little hopeful, but she couldn't force herself to speak.

She tried again to form the words, interrupted by the ding of the elevator arriving and the doors sliding open.

Elena gave her a sad smile.

"Goodnight, Miss Scott."

Her heart fell.

"Goodnight, Elena, please just...be safe?"

She nodded, and Maya watched from her doorway until the elevator doors had closed and she was gone.

*

She had arrived at work the following Monday and found a tub of hot chocolate on her desk—the real kind that you stirred into milk, not the instant kind she usually bought because it was cheap. The gesture had made her chest warm and the pit of her stomach hot, and Maya had spent the last three weeks stupidly arguing with herself over what it meant.

She had woken up Sunday morning beyond mortified at the memory of her boss showing up and helping her drunken self into her apartment. Remembering that soft smile when she'd called Elena gorgeous made her want to cringe and whoop all in one breath.

Again and again, she had tried to find occasion to talk to Elena that first week. She'd stayed late two nights for no reason at all other than to try to catch her alone. The first night she had been on a conference call and by 6:15, Maya had given up and left. The second time she had made it all the way to her office door and was greeted by a soft "Miss Scott" and what she swore was a hopeful smile, only to be promptly interrupted by Margaret.

Since then, she had somehow convinced herself she'd imagined it all, that Elena was just being friendly, a concerned employer, nothing more. There was no way someone like her would actually be interested in someone like Maya; as a charity case perhaps, but not as a partner in the bedroom activities and saccharine sweet scenes she had been imagining the two of them starring in together more and more in her daydreams.

So, one week became two, two became three, and things had been all quiet on the Elena front—radio silence to be exact—and she was still trying to convince herself it was for the best. Still trying not to shamelessly stare and study and memorize Elena whenever she was in her vicinity and failing miserably because she was just so damn fascinated with her.

"Mama, look!"

Livvie held up a page in one of her coloring books, and Maya nodded absentmindedly.

God she was a junkie.

Addicted to the thought of Elena, the idea of something that could never be. Maybe that was it...she just had to prove to herself she was wrong. She had totally read into things that weren't there and Elena wasn't interested in her romantically. Though involved actually communicating with her.

She pulled out her phone, snapped a quick shot of Livvie coloring, remembering how Elena had said she enjoyed the last one, and pressed send before she could change her mind.

The reply was instant.

Please tell her I said hello!

She wrote back, marveling at how easy it was after weeks of sending a simple text, starting a simple conversation, seeming so ridiculously hard.

I will. How are you? Having a good weekend?

The reply came quickly, and Maya remembered that Elena dictated her text messages.

I'm fine. Been at the office waiting all day for the city, other than that it's been typical. You?

Why are you waiting for the city?

She imagined Elena alone at work with a burst pipe or no power, and instantly, she was looking around the room, locating her shoes, ready to go to help.

There's an intruder behind the building.

Maya's heart beat hard, and she was about to jump to her feet and tell Livvie to get her shoes and coat when her phone buzzed again. She clicked the message and staring back at her was a picture of the most pathetic little fluff ball she had ever seen. Hiding behind some sort of cardboard packaging against the dumpster was a black kitten with brilliant green eyes. It looked to be long haired and, always a sucker for cute animals, Maya thought it was adorable.

She jabbed Elena's name on her phone screen, calling her now without thinking twice.

"Hello?"

"You called the city on him?"

"Hello to you, too, Miss Scott."

Maya rolled her eyes.

"Elena, he's just a baby, a cute little kitten baby. Do you know what the pound is like?"

"Well, he can't stay where he is. He's been wailing nonstop. The ground floor staff are complaining."

Maya covered the mouthpiece, taking the phone away from her ear.

"Livvie... Livvie Bug... Liv..."

On the third try, Livvie finally unglued her big green eyes from their current task and turned to her.

"Can you get your shoes, please?"

Elena called her name down the line, and she turned back to her phone conversation, clicking it onto speaker. Bringing up the app, she ordered an Uber.

"Call the city back and tell them he left or something, I'll come by and remove *the intruder* for you."

She looked up, gesturing again for Livvie to go find her shoes, but Livvie still didn't move.

"Hang on one sec, Elena."

Livvie's mischievous eyes lit up at the word, excited.

"Do you want to go see Elena?"

Livvie nodded frantically.

"Then bring me your shoes and your coat, okay?"

She was gone to her room to fetch the items before Maya had even finished speaking.

"And what exactly are you going to do with it, Miss Scott?"

She hadn't really got that far, but the thought of the cute little kitten alone in the pound made her sad and just didn't sit well with her, hitting somehow too close to home.

"I dunno, maybe we'll keep it. Kids do better when they grow up with pets, right?"

"That's not scientifically proven."

Elena didn't sound impressed one bit at the idea. Maya rolled her eyes.

"Just call off the city and we'll be there in twenty."

*

When they arrived at TMF, Maya shot Elena a quick message asking her to meet them out back before she unbuckled Livvie from her car seat and lugged it out of the back of the patient driver's car as she thanked him again. She hadn't mentioned anything about the kitten, not wanting to disappoint Livvie if it had already taken off.

"Is Mm'lena here?"

Livvie craned her head, trying to see past Maya's body and around the mostly deserted garage, already eager to see her friend again.

"Yeah, Bug, she's here. We have to go find her though, okay?"

Livvie set off in search of her, small boots slapping loudly against the concrete floor in her excitement.

"Hold my hand, please," Maya reminded her in her best soothing voice, and even though Livvie did as she asked, she still towed her along, barely giving her time to close the car door and tugging her in the wrong direction before Maya corrected her. They walked the short distance to the elevator. The car seat bumped against Maya's leg with each step.

"Where's Mm'lena, Mama?"

"Almost there, Bug."

They made it down two more floors before the question was repeated.

Mercifully, before Maya had to answer they reached the ground floor, and the doors were swinging open,

Elena waiting for them. Her stoic expression cracked, a smile spilling onto the face as Livvie shrieked and ran for her, yanking her hand from Maya's, who let her go.

"You're here!" Livvie crowed gleefully, and Maya watched for a few minutes as she clung to Elena's leg and they talked excitedly together.

When she finally managed to catch Elena's eye, she gave her an enquiring glance, to which Elena pointedly looked to the left in response. Maya followed her gaze and headed out of the garage to the back of the building.

She heard the cat before she saw it. It was smaller than it sounded, and her heart ached for it, seemingly alone in the world and huddled by the dumpster, terrified.

"Hey, buddy."

It was quiet as she reached for the kitten, and just as it made to run, she grabbed it and scooped it into her arms, talking quietly. She was rewarded with a rumbling purr after a few long seconds of uncertainty. Exhaling, she thought that maybe this wouldn't be so bad.

She returned to where she had left her daughter. Elena saw her first, her eyes fixed on the black bundle in her arms.

"It could have fleas!"

She sounded so scandalized Maya had to laugh.

"What that?" Livvie asked, eyes zeroed in on the little cat like laser beams, and in that moment, Maya knew they would be keeping the thing.

"It's a kitty. He's just a little baby, and he's scared, so we have to be quiet and very gentle with him, okay?"

Livvie rushed over to look, dragging Elena with her. As soon as Livvie released her and raised her hands to touch the animal instead, Elena stepped back.

"Where is hims mama?"

Maya held her daughter's hand with her own, helping her gently pet the cat, somehow acutely aware of Elena's eyes on them as they did so.

"Maybe he got lost, or maybe his parents aren't around anymore." She swallowed thickly, feeling stupid for all the emotions that were invading her chest.

"Elena found him out here all alone, and she thought maybe he could use a new family, so that's why we're here."

Livvie looked between her, Elena, the kitten, and back again. "Maybe he will be our kitty, 'kay, Mm'lena?"

Elena nodded. "I think that would be wonderful, honey, after he gets a bath and the proper immunizations, so he doesn't get sick or make you sick."

She gave Maya a pointed look, to which she was just about to respond when Livvie spoke again, seemingly unaware of or unbothered by Elena's words.

"So, he goes to our home, 'kay? But you comes to visit?"

Elena gave her an award-winning smile, so kind and genuine that Maya melted in response.

"Okay, sweetie."

Livvie took her hand back and comically tiptoed a few paces away from the kitten before she broke into a run and hugged Elena's leg. Maya knew the gesture was her daughter's thanks without words, and she gave Elena an overly dramatic, weary look. How did she get all the glory when she didn't even like the kitten? Elena returned it with an equally overplayed smug smirk, and Maya couldn't help but giggle, an ease in the interaction that felt so familiar—a camaraderie, a domesticity that surprised her. The bubble of happiness around her burst as she wondered if this was making Elena uncomfortable, or sad, remembering how badly she wanted children of her own.

"Okay, Liv, we've taken up enough of Elena's time. Tell her thanks for the kitty, and let's get him home."

She saw the smile on Elena's face falter for the briefest moment, or maybe she imagined it. Either way, she straightened up and stuck out a hand for her daughter, balancing the car seat in the crook of her elbow, the other still holding the kitten, waiting for her to say her goodbyes.

"Thank you for kitty, Mm'lena."

Livvie was still holding tight to Elena's hand, and when she turned those green eyes on her, Maya knew she was about to ask if they could stay or if Elena was coming too. Giving her a look that left no room for arguing, she wiggled her fingers.

"Come on, hold my hand, it's time to call a cab and go home."

Livvie considered it for a few seconds, but thankfully, seemed to give in and skipped over to grab the proffered hand.

Chapter Five

Maya's phone chimed again. Unbothered by the interruption, Livvie continued to turn the pages of the book they had been reading together before bed.

"Thirsty, Mama..."

Maya nodded her understanding, getting up to move to the kitchen. Pausing to lean on the counter, she was pleased to see *Elena* at the top of the new message notification on her cell. Taking a moment, she swiped it open, indulging herself in what had become her guilty pleasure over the last month since Elena had given them the kitten. They texted back and forth a few times a day. Maya mostly sent pictures of the aptly named Midnight and updates on Livvie with occasional remarks about her own day or life. Elena replied with great enthusiasm about Livvie and shared a few snippets of her own world here and there, though she still didn't appear to be wholly convinced about the cat.

Tonight's offering did not disappoint. Staring back at her from the little screen was the caption *Another boring business dinner*...and Elena in what looked like a very expensive off-the-shoulder dress, all dark smoky makeup and a crimson-red lip that made Maya want to run her tongue across its waxy surface.

Catching her own thoughts, alone in her kitchen, she almost blushed. Winling had taken to lightly teasing her about her big fat crush on her boss, and as vehemently as she denied it to them, she knew now, it was true.

Elena was a drug, and the more she tasted her, the more she wanted. She dodged Midnight, who was sleeping inconveniently smack bang in the middle of the kitchen floor, and opened the fridge to grab some water for her daughter.

A loud crash interrupted her thoughts, guilt turning to panic in a millisecond as she rushed back to Livvie's small bedroom in the tiny apartment she rented.

Livvie was already crying, the bookcase on the floor, books around her, one arm clutched to her chest as she screamed at a pitch that terrified Maya instantly.

"Livvie?"

Maya rushed over to her and tried to quiet the hysterical sobs that were stealing her breath. She took in the scene and realized with a sickening jolt that Livvie had tried to climb up to get a book, bringing the whole bookcase crashing down on her—the bookcase Maya was meant to secure to the wall after the move and had totally forgotten about.

"Where does it hurt?"

She questioned her daughter as softly as she could, her own panic forcing tears into her eyes. When she finally pried Livvie's right arm from her chest it hung at an angle that made Maya feel nauseous.

"Okay, Bug, we'll get you fixed, it's okay."

Not knowing what else to do, and terrified out of her mind, Maya wrapped Livvie's injured limb in a sheet. She pressed it back against Livvie's chest and rocked her as she cried while, with her other hand, she dialed an ambulance.

*

The ambulance ride was a blur of red and blue and tears soaking her jeans, and Maya was lost somewhere between panic and guilt and a soul-shattering despair that her daughter was hurt.

The wait by the gurney had been short, and then Livvie was taken back, through doors to a room where Maya was not allowed to follow. She knew down to her bones that it was because the staff knew her position. She might be Livvie's mother, but she was not her legal guardian, and so, she was relegated just to wait.

With tears dry on her cheeks and her long hair in a lopsided messy ponytail, she tried to pull herself together, to be better, to handle this like a real mother would— would she ever feel like she was worthy to be one?

She forced herself not to cry and asked herself what the responsible thing to do was now. It was late Sunday evening, and she remembered she had work tomorrow. She needed to stay with Livvie, if Holt would let her, so happy to have something to do, she pulled out her cell. Ignoring the picture of beautiful Elena still smiling out at her after she unlocked the screen, she clicked off the message and called her instead.

When the line rang and rang and went to voicemail, she left a message. By the time she was done, she couldn't even remember what she had said, so apologizing one more time that she maybe wouldn't make it into the office tomorrow and promising to update her as soon as possible, she ended the call.

Pacing was the only way to make the waiting bearable, Livvie's pained sobs still chasing her in her mind, up and down the length of the waiting room. So, she waited, and she paced, looking right through the nurses who passed by, and the occasional patient who offered her a smile.

The door at the end of the hall banged open. The sound was too loud in the quiet, a gunshot through the haze of her panic, and then Elena was striding unsteadily toward her, still wearing that beautiful dress from the picture, and Maya struggled to react through the thick fog she was swimming in.

"Maya."

Shaking hands were on her face and eyes brimming with concern were searching hers.

"El...Elena, what... You're here?" Her voice sounded weak and pitchy and far-off even to her own ears, and when Elena tugged her along in the direction of the handicap bathroom, she followed without a fight, her mind still not caught up with the fact that she was here.

The door was closed behind them, and then Elena was close to her, so close under the harsh fluorescents, pushing her to perch on the edge of the counter, squeezing her upper arms until finally, she was falling, falling, back to Earth, and able to take a breath.

"Your voicemail, you sounded terrible, and I just wanted to help."

Elena's back was to her, the bag she strode in with on the floor, and suddenly, her dress had followed.

Faced with black lace lingerie, and oh God, yes, those were suspenders, Maya had no idea where to look, so she stared at the ceiling instead and ached to know if Livvie was okay.

Moments passed and then Elena's hands were jumping on her knees, and she tilted her head forward until they locked eyes.

"What happened?"

Her voice was soft but strong, and somehow, with Elena here, Maya felt like she could survive this. Elena was dressed again in a soft cashmere sweater and jeans, and somewhere distant in her mind Maya thought she had never been more beautiful.

"We were reading, I went to get her a drink, and she tried to climb the bookshelf for a book. I think it fell... Her arm was... It's..." Sobs erupted, and then she was clasped against Elena, held so tight that, somehow, she was able to breathe.

Elena rocked them side to side, partly thanks to her CP, and partly by conscious choice. At least that's how it felt, and Maya clung to her.

"Maya, it was not your fault. Accidents happen. Look at me, I'm the poster girl for an accident and its consequences."

From the little bit of reading on CP that Maya had done, she knew Elena was referring to whatever had caused her to develop it, and she was able to share a watery laugh with her.

"Livvie is going to need you, okay?" Tissues were thrust into her hand, and Maya was drying her eyes as requested. A splash of water on her face felt good, and a cool hand squeezing her clammy one felt better, and then she was being led back out into the waiting room.

"Did they take her back?"

She nodded the affirmative and waited for Elena to ask why she wasn't with her daughter back there. She just didn't have the stomach to explain it all, to tell that story, not tonight. Mercifully, Elena stayed silent beside her, a sentry to ward off the panic that had consumed her prior to her arrival.

Robert Holt burst through the door fifteen minutes later, a teary-eyed Bella hot on his heels.

"What did you do?" He was hissing before he even reached her, moving faster than a man of his age on a cane should be able, and Maya felt herself shrinking, shrinking, shrinking, as she always did under his gaze. "These weekends we give you are a courtesy, Maya, and now it seems you've proven you're not even fit for that."

"Robert."

Elena's voice interrupted, rough but strong, and it was then Maya realized they were still holding hands, Elena's tan fingers clasped tight around her own, in the same moment she saw Robert's eyes flash down to notice it too.

"How nice to see you. I had no idea you were Livvie's grandfather." Her tone was polite but cool and all business, and thankful that Robert's attention wasn't still on her, his cruel blue eyes promising to take away everything she loved, Maya stayed silent beside her.

"Elena—"

Robert was caught off balance. She could almost hear the falter in his voice, taste the trepidation with which he said her name, and Maya clung to it like a life raft, because for the first time in three years, Holt didn't seem quite so untouchable.

"Maya's had quite the fright as you can see. She's very shaken up. Complete accident, as sometimes happens with children." The last word was slurred, and Maya glanced to Elena, knowing the slip would have been embarrassing for someone as proud as her, though if it was, she didn't let it show.

"You know what happened?" Holt was asking, talking, discussing, like a reasonable human being, and the spectacle almost blew Maya's mind.

"Yes, but I think Maya can explain it better. Go ahead, sweetheart."

The endearment shocked her aching heart, setting it daring to beat again for the first time since the thud of Livvie's bookcase falling that felt so long ago.

"She climbed the bookcase while I was fetching her a drink before bed. I've told her a hundred times to wait for me." She trailed off dumbly, fighting the urge to apologize, because she deserved this, she deserved the reaming out she knew was coming. She deserved the sneering; the failure she knew she would see reflected in his angry eyes.

"Maya called an ambulance right away and I met them here. Livvie's in the back being attended to. Seems like a broken arm, we're still waiting to hear from the doctor." Elena took control of the situation effortlessly, and Maya was endlessly grateful.

Without a word, Holt stormed off to the nurse's station, no doubt to raise hell, and Maya felt the warm weight of a very pregnant Bella settling down beside her on the seats. Bella slipped a gentle hand into the free one that wasn't holding Elena's.

"I'm so glad you're both okay, Maya. I'm sure Livvie will be all right."

Somehow, she was able to nod and offer Bella a watery smile, taking the squeeze Elena offered her through their entwined fingers and letting it lift her up, tug her through, carry her forward and give her the strength to hold on, to survive until she could see Livvie and know for sure she was okay.

She tried to ignore the nurse explaining loudly that she hadn't been allowed to go back with Livvie as she wasn't her legal guardian, and that Robert would need to sign the paperwork so she could get her cast. She couldn't stop herself shaking. Elena's body rocked harder and harder next to her, too, reminding Maya of a spinning top, a coiling spring, a shaken soda, ready to blow.

She held it together until Robert was accompanied back, Bella following along with an apologetic glance as they went to see her daughter, and then, Maya exploded.

Soundless sobs spiraled into horrible, hacking cries, her body jumping under the force of them. For the first time in years, Maya let someone other than Winling see her really cry, having little choice in the matter. Failure and guilt and worry and doubt swallowed her and spun her around, and the sporadic jerking of Elena's body as she held her tight against her chest was the only thing keeping them from drowning her.

She had no idea how long she cried into Elena's neck, cool fingers soft in her hair, smooth sweater wet against her cheek. Her tears were just beginning to run dry when a nurse interrupted.

"Miss Scott, Mister Holt has given permission for you to go back now if you'd like to see your daughter."

And God she felt dirty, she felt wrong, criminal, an unfit mother who had lost her child, and in that moment she hated Holt, the broken system, and the stupid snotty nurse, but Elena tugged on her hand and helped her to her feet, and all that dissolved in the face of finally being able to see Livvie.

"Mama?" Her heart soared and broke, burst and mended. When they entered the room, a bleary-eyed Livvie was reaching for her with one hand, the other arm in a thick purple cast and strapped across her chest.

"Hi, Bug, hi... You've been so brave."

Maya bent to hug her daughter, who was still sleepy from whatever medication they had given her.

"Mm'lena?"

Looking up with wet eyes, Maya followed Livvie's green ones, so much like her own, up to the woman who had undoubtedly saved her that night.

"Hello, Livvie." Elena's eyes shone with pride that she had been remembered and somehow, even in the face of all that had happened, it was enough to make Maya smile, the first slivers of relief finally finding her after hours of sheer panic.

"We have tea party with my mama and my grampa and Bella and Midnight?"

"Not today, honey." Elena stepped closer, her dark gaze full of so much kindness, as Livvie summoned her until both she and Maya had fingers clasped in one of Livvie's small hands.

"We go home now, Mama?"

Maya ached to say yes, but she already knew Holt would never let that happen. A new fear twisted into her gut—what if he stopped her visits because of this?

"I think you'll be coming home with us tonight, Olivia." Holt cut in.

"You must be tired, Robert, and poor Bella, how far along are you now?" Elena barely nodded as Bella filled in that she was thirty-three weeks.

"It's been a long night. Why don't you take your wife home to rest? I can make sure Maya and Livvie get home safely, and I'm sure Maya wouldn't mind you picking her up tomorrow. She already called in to work, isn't that right, sweetheart?"

There it was again, that endearment. It left Maya dumbstruck, so she simply nodded, desperate for whatever Elena was trying to accomplish to allow her to keep Livvie to come to pass. She needed one more night with her, just to hold her and watch her sleep and know she was really safe.

"I had no idea you were dating again, Miss Scott." Robert's voice was sharp, and Maya recognized his annoyance at the matter, lurking behind his politician's façade. "How nice for you. Elena, please give Cara my best regards."

He ground the words out, and Elena tipped her head cordially, and Maya could hardly believe what was happening.

"We'll pick her up at eleven tomorrow. Goodnight, Miss Scott." He cast a last glance at Livvie, who had fallen asleep still clinging to a handful of her and Elena's fingers, before he and Bella turned to depart.

Elena's arm felt strong around her waist as she answered for them both.

"Goodnight, Robert, Bella. Get home safely."

*

They were discharged from the hospital with a handful of instructions and scenarios to look out for that Maya couldn't remember. Thankfully, Elena had recorded the nurse explaining it all on her phone. As soon as they had arrived home, they had gotten Livvie to bed.

Elena's presence was soothing, and just knowing she wasn't alone with the weight of the day, Maya was able to get her tired daughter through her bedtime routine fairly quickly and painlessly. With it finally done, she flopped down on her sofa, exhausted. Relief washed over her—Livvie was home, and she was going to be okay—followed by a crashing realization that Elena Mars was sitting beside her in her crappy two-bedroom apartment, privy to all her life failings.

"Oh my God, you were at a business dinner. I'm so sorry, Elena."

"Nonsense." Elena took her hand and squeezed it tight between her shaking ones. Apparently, holding hands was something they did now, and Maya could not say she minded one bit.

"I'm so glad you came though."

Elena nodded. "You sounded like you were in a pretty bad state on the voice message, and besides, the dinner was terrible. I was glad to leave."

Maya nodded, returning the secret smile Elena offered.

"You know Robert?"

Elena stiffened but answered.

"Yes, he's a longtime friend of my parents. I'm sorry you have to deal with him. I know he can be a very manipulative little man."

The anger in Elena's tone surprised her, and Maya wondered if it would be prying to want to know why she felt that way, though Elena continued before she had to ask.

"Before my mother finally accepted the fact that I'm a lesbian, she would set me up on dates with men she deemed...suitable for me. Robert Holt was one of them."

"He's like forty years older than us!" Maya interjected, angrier than she thought she ought to be that Elena had been forced to go on a date with anyone, let alone the man who had ruined her life.

"Only twenty years older than me, dear. You forget I'm fourteen years your senior." Elena's eyes seemed to twinkle at this, and Maya wondered what it meant, wondered if the age gap mattered to her, or if she enjoyed the thought just a little bit like Maya knew she secretly did herself.

"Anyway, after the first date when I refused to see him again, Robert tried to blackmail me. I won't go into details, but thankfully, I had my mother put an end to it. Of course, there was a price, but isn't there always."

It wasn't a question, really, and Maya squeezed their joined hands. Listening to Elena talk about her clearly less than perfect family made her feel a little better about her own checkered past, a little less messy next to Elena who looked effortlessly gorgeous in her casual clothes, and rocked every business meeting like she was born a CEO.

"I appreciate you standing up to him for us."

The dim light from the hallway cast a soft glow across Elena's features, and when she turned to look at her through the darkness, their eyes meeting, the sight stole Maya's breath. How did this woman not realize how desirable she was?

"I'm sorry he assumed we were involved."

Maya snickered at her choice of wording, and Elena rolled her eyes.

"Very mature, Miss Scott." The title was playful, and Maya found she liked it more that way.

"It just seemed like the easiest means to an end. It wasn't my intention, but he assumed, and it worked, so correcting him seemed futile."

"Elena... You don't have to explain. I didn't mind."

The words were soft, something swelling between them, and Maya was feeling everything all in one breath, butterflies dancing in her stomach and that magnetic pull she knew was screaming *kiss me, kiss me.*

"You didn't?" The question was repeated back to her, quiet and rough, and she shook her head.

They studied each other for a long moment, Maya's breathing loud in her own ears, her eyes falling to Elena's lips, still stained the faintest of crimson. Just as she was daring herself to lean in, Elena spoke.

"You've had a long night. I should let you get some rest."

Rejection hit her hard and hot in the gut, and she nodded, tearing her eyes away and pushing up from her seat, taking her hand back from Elena's cool grip in the process.

"Maya." Elena's voice was soft as she struggled to her own feet. The pads of her fingers grazed Maya's cheek as she pushed a loose strand of blonde hair back from her face. "You've been through the wringer tonight. You need to rest and recuperate." Her hand lingered just beneath her ear, those dark eyes holding a thousand promises that Maya was too scared to name, though the words did soothe the sting of the rejection some.

She followed Elena dutifully to the door, suddenly bone-tired and ready for her bed.

"Goodnight, Miss Scott."

She was opening her mouth to return the sentiment when Elena's soft lips brushed her cheek. Elena jerked slightly against her, making one kiss become two, before she was pulling away.

With a smile on her face, Maya watched her make her way back down the corridor to the elevator.

"Goodnight, Elena."

*

It was midday Monday before Maya made it into the office. Livvie had woken up happier than she had expected and milked her shiny new purple cast for all the "one more story" and breakfasts in bed it was worth.

Robert was surprisingly civil when he came to collect her, and when she arrived at work and found Kevin was mercifully absent with the flu, it was shaping up to be a fine day after a very rocky weekend...until Margaret informed her Elena was out of the office, and Maya's mood plummeted.

By Tuesday she was riddled with guilt, sure the night spent at the hospital followed by driving them home and taking care of them both had taken too much out of Elena. She wondered if Elena was sick, or just exhausted, and was suddenly struck with the realization that she knew very little about Elena at all—where she lived, if she had anyone to take care of her, or even check on her?

She arrived at work ridiculously early, enjoying the less busy journey on the bus, and resolving for it to be one of her last. This weekend had proven to her beyond doubt that she needed a car, and she planned to get one. Waiting at her desk, every time the elevator dinged, Maya's eyes shot up, disappointed, until finally Elena arrived.

Elena was unreadable in a black wool coat and high-heeled boots, her usual business makeup, and hair styled to perfection. Their eyes met for moment, something soft and secret flashing between them and making Maya's stomach flip, before Elena was heading for her office, staggering slightly yet somehow, still managing to strut.

The workday was quiet, and almost everyone on the floor stopped by her desk to ask about Livvie. Margaret gave her a crocheted winter hat and scarf set she had made for Livvie that turned Maya's eyes glassy. She had never worked with people who actually cared; never felt valued like she did at TMF.

The clicking of Elena's heels across the floor rang out as she headed for lunch, and Maya must have been on her own break when she returned because she never saw her come back, though Margaret scurried off to her office to talk with her throughout the day.

Maya barely waited until the office had cleared before leaving her desk and making a beeline for Elena's. She paused before she rounded the doorframe, stopped by the sound of Elena's voice and a name she knew too well.

"We both know Robert Holt is not to be trusted, Mother. Besides, my personal life is none of his business... Yes."

There was a long pause, presumably while Elena's mother spoke, and Maya became acutely aware she was eavesdropping, glancing guiltily over her shoulder back to where the others were still packing up for the night. Just as she was debating walking away Elena spoke again.

"I don't need a date for the party, I'm quite capable of finding my... What?" Another pregnant silence and then Elena ground out her last words. "Fine, we can discuss it at lunch. Yes. Goodnight, Mother."

Maya heard the heavy exhale that followed the thud of a cell phone being tossed on a desk, and she waited a few more seconds before stepping into the office, trying to ignore the guilt that was eating at her over more than the amount of time Elena had spent on her this week.

"Maya..." Elena said her name on an exhale. Her tone sounded like relief, and she wasn't sure she'd ever heard it sound better.

"Hi, I just wanted to see how you were. I don't feel like I thanked you properly for Sunday night, and you weren't here yesterday. I was worried."

Elena's eyes were glowing, and that soft smile Maya was becoming increasingly besotted with played on Elena's mouth. Her neck jerked, the movement slurring her speech as she replied, but Maya barely noticed.

"You were worried about me?"

"Of course, I was."

She sat without an invitation, the pull to be closer to Elena stronger than the old etiquette that somehow didn't seem to apply to her anymore.

"Well... Thank you, I'm quite all right. I had a meeting to attend yesterday. How's Livvie?"

Maya recounted her Monday morning as her daughter's willing slave, and Elena laughed along gleefully, her face full of adoring mirth Maya had never dreamed she would see in someone else's eyes for her own kid.

"And Robert, was he civil?"

"Yes, very, I don't know what you did to him, but he didn't say a thing. No threatening to stop my visits, no underhanded comments about what an unfit mother I am." She laughed off the pain of the words at her own expense, but Elena just watched her stoically.

"Maya, you obviously love Livvie very much, you were devastated this weekend, and you didn't deserve to be treated like anything other than a terrified mother whose child was hurt."

The words struck her in the gut, and she wanted to cry because she didn't remember the last time she had felt so validated. Yes, it was stupid to need to hear it, but she did, and somehow coming from Elena, it counted, so much.

She managed to squeeze out a raspy thank-you, choking the tears back down with a thick swallow. For a second, she thought Elena was going to reach across the desk and take her hand, and she wanted her to. Instead, Elena's gaze flitted to the open door behind her head, and her hands remained in place, shaking in her lap.

The silence stretched too long, but Maya was loath to end their meeting, fiddling with the sleeves of her haphazardly thrown on leather jacket, trying to find the right words.

"Thank you." She looked up and hoped her eyes were conveying what her mouth wasn't. "I don't think I would have survived Sunday without you. I'm sorry you left your dinner. Maybe we can go out to dinner and I can make it up to you?"

That was not planned, and the words surprised her as much as she was sure they surprised Elena who was suddenly smiling her predatory smile again, all dark eyes and sharp white teeth, and an intensity that made Maya's insides quiver.

"Are you offering to take me out for dinner, Miss Scott?"

That voice should be illegal.

"Yes?" God, she hadn't meant for it to come out like a question, pitchy with nerves like a twelve-year-old boy asking his crush to the dance. Her cheeks burned.

"Friday?"

Maya could only nod. Elena was in her element, that devious smile still playing on her lips, her eyes twin molten embers Maya was sure were devouring her whole as they roamed her face, down her neck, over her exposed collarbones in a path she could almost physically feel the echo of on her skin.

Elena was an enigma. In that moment Maya remembered the fractured woman looking down at Livvie and being so convinced nobody would ever want a life with her, yet faced with what Maya was pretty sure was a date, she was all sultriness and sex and freaking irresistible. Did Elena think she wasn't desirable beyond sex?

Looking back, holding eyes turned obsidian with her own, she resolved to find out.

Chapter Six

The week had been terrifying. From Livvie's accident, to asking Elena out to dinner, to finally taking a significant chunk from her savings and buying a car, Maya had worried, a lot. Most of that hardly compared to the worry she faced standing on the doorstep of what she could only describe as a mansion, checking the address on her text messages again, and wondering if she had gotten the right place.

"Maya." Elena breathed out her name, and she glanced up to find the heavy wooden door open and Elena standing in its frame looking absolutely radiant.

Glowing tan skin, soft dark makeup perfect around her eyes, and her hair straight around her shoulders. A dark-emerald dress clung to Elena's body, falling off one shoulder and leaving her collarbones bare. The thin black choker around Elena's neck made Maya lick her lips, and God she was glad she had worn the only little black dress she owned, knowing it displayed her assets to their best effect.

"Elena, you look beautiful." She was cliché but she had no idea how else to frame the absolute truth of her words. If through some monumental misconception Elena wasn't thinking of this as a date, she had to know that Maya was now.

"As do you. I must say, you clean up nicely. A welcome change from all that leather and denim."

Her foot tapped against the stoop as she spoke, and Maya noticed her usual shaking seemed to be amplified, her left arm actually bumping her side as it bounced.

She stepped back, giving Elena space to slip into her coat, and reached up to pull it onto her shoulders without thinking. Her hands hovered a little too long on Elena's slim frame, until Elena looked back over her shoulder, dark eyes full of a million promises, and Maya swallowed hard and stepped away.

"Of course, you bought a Mustang." Elena rolled her eyes as Maya opened the door and helped her down into the seat, ignoring the glare the action earned her. She wasn't doing it because of Elena's CP.

"Be nice to Ladybug, please." Elena scoffed and Maya closed the door, watching her through the glass as she jerkily worked to reach behind herself for her seatbelt. She rushed around the front of her new car and slid down into the driver's seat, still feeling a sliver of excitement at taking the wheel.

"This is exactly why you don't let your three-year-old name your sexy new car."

Elena threw her head back and laughed, and they were on their way.

*

With her eyes on the leather-bound menu, Maya tried not to baulk at the prices, thanking God she had already transferred some funds from her savings account to cover the cost of the evening. She had tried to choose a restaurant she thought Elena would like, thankful now that in the end she had just copped out and made a reservation at an absurdly expensive one and hoped for the best.

"Before we begin, I want to make it clear I'm paying for the evening—well, the Mars Fund is." Elena's voice was rich and smooth, and she didn't look up from her menu as Maya closed hers.

"Elena, this is my way of saying thank-you. Really, dinner is the least I can do."

Elena offered her a wry smile. "Your presence is more than enough, dear. I have a ridiculously large budget for business dinners and entertaining, and it would be very nice to use it for something I may actually enjoy for once."

Elena's eyes held hers and Maya could feel the beginnings of a blush on her cheeks, before finally, she relented with a nod.

"Good evening, ladies."

Their server appeared, and she instantly reminded Maya of a Caucasian Winling, all lean androgynous charm and a fitted black slacks and vest combo while the other female servers wore skirts.

Elena ordered some fancy French-sounding wine with what Maya would wager was an almost perfect accent, and of course, a salad.

Suddenly unsure about her original choice of steak, Maya decided to play it safe and ask for a pasta dish with the house red, not missing the irritating way their server's eyes lingered on Elena appreciatively, though she could hardly blame her.

Either totally oblivious or uncaring, Elena saw the server away, returning their menus with a smoky grin, before she reached a shaking hand across the table, snapping Maya out of what she realized abruptly had been her staring.

"Are you all right?"

Elena's fingers were cold against her own, and Maya almost wrapped them in her hand before she thought better of it. Holding hands at the hospital seemed so long ago now, and she was suddenly unsure.

"Yes, sorry, just thinking."

Elena nodded, seeming to sense some seriousness in the moment and choosing a topic accordingly.

"I've been meaning to ask you, and you don't have to answer if you don't want to, about how you came to be involved with Robert Holt?"

Maya's stomach dropped. Elena's fingers rested against the back of her hand, bumping her knuckles as they shook, giving her the strength to resurrect that story. Elena seemed to sense her hesitance.

"We really don't have to talk about it, I just... I had wondered if you were his daughter. I only ever heard of him having a son who passed away a few years back, but I couldn't fit it together any other way."

Maya grit her teeth, blowing out a quiet exhale and steeling herself. Elena was going to find out eventually, and so far, she had been nothing but supportive, never judgmental, despite how Maya knew the custody situation must look from the outside.

"It's fine, I um... Well." She fumbled over where to start, saved by the server returning with their drinks and pausing for a moment to talk to Elena about the wine. As frustrating as the server's presence was, it gave her a much-needed moment to collect herself.

When Elena turned back to her, she was ready, though she sorely missed the soft weight of Elena's hand over her own.

"My parents died in a head-on collision when I was fifteen." She pushed on quickly, studying the table, not wanting to give Elena a chance to interject, to pity her. "I went into care until I was seventeen, group homes mostly. Nobody wants to adopt a kid that close to college age." She tried to joke, but it fell flat, even to her own ears. "I met Neal Holt while I was in one of those homes. He was the social worker for another kid and ten years older than me. Somehow, we became friends. He helped me get my life on track, get out of the system, and by the time I was eighteen, I had applied to college and was set to leave in the fall to study journalism. I wanted to tell stories that mattered."

She laughed softly at her past self, her naivety, and finally risked a glance up to see an impassive Elena watching her carefully, her face set into an unreadable mask as she waited for her to continue.

"I um…" She forced herself not to wilt under Elena's gaze. "We met again just after my first semester at college at some party. I was pretty sure by then I liked women, but Neal had been so kind to me; I was drinking, and I—"

She stalled, picking at her nails, trying to find the words to stumble through this part of the story, the part that always tripped her up because even her own private thoughts on it were still muddy and uncertain and something she rarely touched.

A strong hand pulled hers apart, fastening its grip around her fingers and squeezing, waiting, though the silence wasn't expectant. Elena offered her an encouraging smile, and swallowing, she continued.

"I didn't say no, but I didn't exactly say yes, you know? It wasn't… He didn't… So um, three months later I found out I was pregnant with Livvie. I had Neal's number. We'd texted from time to time. He had apologized after that night and said it was a mistake. I just sort of brushed it off. He was a good guy, and it was done, so... Anyway, they called me..."

Her eyes grew wet, unshed tears thick in her throat, and she swallowed them down, focusing on a single spot of white table linen, trying not to blink and let any fall.

"I got a call that Neal was found dead, suicide. I guess he felt guilty about what happened, and that's what I first heard from Robert Holt. I was nineteen and pregnant, terrified. I was missing classes, and my scholarship was based on track, which of course was out for at least a year while I was having the baby. My life was spiraling out of control."

"Maya..." Elena's voice was tender, soft, loving in a way Maya knew she couldn't let get inside her because in that moment, it would break her, shatter her into a thousand pieces. She had started, and somehow, she had to finish. As much as she hated this story, it was cathartic, letting it out, and part of her just wanted Elena to know. She wanted to show her the dirtiest, most damaged parts of herself and let her go ahead and run now if she was going to. It would hurt less that way.

"Robert wanted to take the baby. He said he could give her the best life when she was born, that she was all that was left of Neal. He was a complete stranger to me, and I had no idea if he was even a good person, so I said no. I was arrested two months later for a huge batch of meth they found in my room, enough to make it look like I was dealing. Livvie was born while I was doing six months in prison. Holt won custody. I've been trying to get her back ever since while he keeps me right where he wants me."

She was empty by the end, numb but relieved it was over. She didn't dare to look up and see Elena's face; she didn't want to be crushed by what she found there.

"In case you were wondering the drugs weren't mine."

A hiss from across the table and a tug on her hand that felt intentional rather than the background movement of Elena's CP forced her eyes up to meet Elena's blazing dark gaze.

"Holt is a snake. He uses what he has to work any system to his advantage and thinks he can buy or bully his way to whatever he wants." Elena sounded furious. "I'm so sorry, Maya. Have you tried to fight the charges?"

She shook her head. "You said it yourself, he always wins. Every time I get on my feet, he kicks me back down, gets me fired, evicted... After I stopped talking about trying to get custody of Livvie, he backed off some, but when he showed up with her at the office, I wondered if he was going to start again."

Elena looked furious, murderous, and Maya was touched by her concern, but she didn't dare believe it would make any difference. She had tried so hard not to dwell on the way Holt had backed down to Elena at the hospital, not to let it foster any hope in her, because having it crushed again would be just too painful.

"Are you going to file for custody?" Somehow coming from Elena, the question didn't feel like prying, not like pushing as it so often did when Winling asked. It was genuine as a question, and all she felt she had to give was her honest response.

"I don't know. With Robert she will go to an amazing private school, be able to do tons of extracurriculars, and I know Bella loves her..."

"Maya Scott, you can do this. If you want to, and if you choose to, you could give her an amazing life, too, with her mother who loves her very much. Don't you dare sell yourself short in comparison to him."

"I do want it. I am going to try." She was finally brave enough to commit. She had been working toward filing for custody for so long that when she finally arrived at a point where she was ready—decent home, good job, financially stable—she was too scared to take the next step. Elena's vote of confidence made her brave because under the influence of the woman she could practically feel believing in her, she, too, dared to believe that just maybe, she could fight Robert and win.

A simple nod and Elena seemed to simmer down, a raging inferno slipping back to a slower boil, though her dark eyes were still steely and determined.

"Good. When you're ready, one of my closest friends is an excellent family lawyer, one of the best in the state I believe. I'd like to give her your number?"

It took a gargantuan effort not to baulk, and Elena must have seen it on her face.

"How about I just give you her number and you can call her when you're ready? I'll make sure she's expecting you."

Maya nodded at that. Elena gave her hand one last squeeze and let it go.

"Good, now drink your wine and tell me where on Earth you found that awful leather jacket you insist on wearing to work every day, despite the fact it's freezing outside."

She couldn't help but laugh at Elena's candor, so, relieved for a break in the tension, she took a long sip of her drink, and tried to let the heaviness in her chest from their previous topic go.

"Are you always so bossy over dinner, Miss Mars?"

Elena grasped her playful tone immediately, leaning forward in her seat and licking her lips.

"Well, Miss Scott, that depends entirely on who I'm *eating out* with."

The words sounded pornographic, and Maya let out an embarrassing little squeak as she inhaled sharply in response. She half expected Elena to laugh, but she was just watching her with predatory eyes that were doing nothing to slow her racing heart.

Just when she was sure she was going to expire from the thorough eye-fucking Elena was shamelessly giving her, she was saved by their chipper server delivering their food.

Shyly pushing her pasta around her plate, unsure how to start up conversation again after...that, Maya noticed Elena staring down at her salad.

"Did they get your order wrong?"

"Yes, I ordered the chopped chicken breast."

Maya eyed the definitely whole piece of meat on her plate and was about to jokingly tell her to *just chop it up then, princess,* when she realized the problem and caught herself in time.

Looking at Elena's shaking hands, the moment suddenly fraught, she felt her frustration.

"Would you like to try some of the pasta? It's delicious, and I can take care of the chicken for you and maybe steal a bite?" She attempted to make the offer in the most casual, least humiliating way possible. She knew she hadn't entirely succeeded, but when Elena gave her a nod and a quiet "very well," she leaned over and switched their plates.

"What do you think?"

She hurried to keep conversation flowing as she quickly and carefully chopped the offending chicken into manageable chunks. She stuffed a healthy bite of it into her mouth before she put down her cutlery and prepared to pass the plate back.

"I think you're beautiful."

She almost choked.

"Swallow, Miss Scott."

She did so obediently, licking the last of the dressing from her lips before passing Elena's dish back and retrieving her own.

Dinner continued as smoothly as it had before, conversation falling back into easier territory, though Maya never did fully recover from the compliment that had caught her completely off guard.

Even as she smiled and laughed and spilled more than a bit of salad on the fancy table linen, Elena had her totally enraptured. Those dark eyes could set her body burning at will. Maya wondered how the hell she had ever tried to deny that she was insanely attracted to this woman.

"I trust everything was delicious?"

The dapper server swooped back in, all hundred-kilowatt smile and cute bow tie, and Maya stewed quietly as she talked exclusively with Elena, her annoyance boiling over as Elena's fingers gripped the server's arm as they shared a joke she hadn't cared to listen to.

"Excuse me, I'll be right back."

Elena barely seemed to have heard her, still busy with the server, and shame-faced, Maya rushed to the bathroom.

It made no sense. Elena was always so attentive, she had been so supportive and made her interest apparent, yet in the brighter lighting of the bathroom, Maya could see clearly. A woman like Elena could never want her, not really, not broken little Maya Scott, with her felony and her teen pregnancy and the daughter she wasn't good enough to keep. Tears rose in her throat again, and she'd almost cried far too many times already for a week, let alone one single night.

Steeling herself, she reached up and fixed a strand of loosely curled hair back behind her ear, looking at her face, softly made up, her fancy outfit and high, high heels—the costume of a pretender. These expensive restaurants would never be her life, and she was a fool to think she could be part of Elena's world.

The door opened and Elena appeared behind her, her expression stormy, and when they locked eyes in the mirror Maya's throat ran dry.

"There you are... I wondered where you went in such a hurry."

Maya licked her parched lips, ready to offer some polite half-truth, when suddenly Elena was in her space, her front pressed against Maya's back, forcing her hips forward against the sink. The scent of her perfume was intoxicating.

"Did that make you jealous, Maya?"

And there it was again, that voice, dark and dangerous, her lips caressing every syllable of Maya's name as it fell from her mouth.

Shame spilled hot into her gut because yes, it had, but arousal followed close on its heels, her body aching shamelessly for Elena just to devour her right there in the very classy public restroom.

"Yes."

The word was barely a whisper, her gaze fixed on the white porcelain, not daring to look up, feeling the moment swelling, a frenzied crescendo speeding toward them like a freight train.

Jerky hands ran up her sides and over the bottom of her ribcage until Elena had two firm hands settled over her breasts almost roughly. The sensation made her arch her back, pushing her hips harder into the sink, her head snapping up before falling back onto Elena's shoulder.

"Is this what you wanted?"

They locked eyes in the mirror again, and Elena let her watch as her lips caressed the shell of her ear with every word, the rocking of her hips pushing Maya's into the sink, and *holy fuck yes.*

Elena laughed, a dirty, dark sound, and she realized she had answered out loud, *shit.*

Glossy dark hair fell over Elena's shoulder, obscuring her face as she bent her head. Maya was already leaning to the side to give her access, her heart thundering, her insides molten, straining, heat surging into her stomach and the point on her neck where she was sure Elena was about to kiss her.

"Elena, darling, I thought it was you."

The door swung open, and Maya almost fell when the pressure of Elena's body left her back. Her lungs deflated with a frantic breath of *no, no, no,* the burn between her thighs making her wonder how she had any blood left for the blush she sensed blooming across her cheeks.

"Mother, what a pleasant surprise."

The greeting was a bucket of ice water over the fire of her arousal. Elena's careful annunciation, the kind she used in the office, immediately made Maya nervous.

"Oh, and you're with a friend. Cara Mars."

Maya half expected to be offered a hand to shake, but Cara only studied her with a condescending look she knew very well from seeing it on Robert's face so many times.

"Mother, this is Maya Scott, we work together at the foundation."

"Yes, darling, I know all about that. Well, I assume your evening is over. Won't you come and sit with your father and me, have some dessert perhaps or maybe just a coffee?"

She watched in disbelief as Cara Mars eyed Elena's midsection like there was any reason at all to be found there why she shouldn't have a dessert—her figure was perfect. Elena turned to her, dark eyes apologetic, and Maya fixed a smile on her face.

"Of course, you should spend some time with your parents. I had a wonderful evening. See you Monday?"

Elena nodded glumly, and Maya was glad she hadn't bought a purse as she booked it for the door.

The Mars women followed behind as she left the restroom. The last thing she heard was Cara Mars speaking to her daughter.

"Stand up straight, and do try to control all that jolting around, Elena. Fancy running into you like this. Your father will be absolutely thrilled."

Chapter Seven

The work week had been a series of infuriating missed connections and embarrassingly erotic dreams, and by Friday, Maya promised herself that come hell or high water she *would* talk to Elena tonight before leaving work.

Though they had exchanged texts, Elena apologizing profusely for her mother's unwelcome interruption, neither of them had braved the subject of what was happening or was about to happen before she had arrived. For her part, Maya was desperate to revisit that thought.

Kevin was back, but seemed subdued, and she was grateful she could easily wave him off when five o'clock finally arrived, having had little interaction with him all day. Smoothing down the patterned dress she had chosen that morning while remembering Elena's comment about her denim and leather—her beloved jacket was still slung over her arm—she collected her check from Margaret's desk as was their Friday custom.

She almost didn't open the little envelope, familiar by now with what the stub would say. When she did, her stomach lurched before it settled. There had to have been a mix-up.

"Margaret, someone in HR made a mistake."

She held out her check, but Margaret didn't even look up from her frantic typing.

"No, honey, that's right. Your pay grade changed. Any issues see Elena." Margaret offered her a quick smile before she returned to whatever she was doing, and suddenly, Maya was furious.

Her boots clunked noisily as she stalked down the hall, but she didn't care. Elena's door was open, and she let herself in, not waiting for her to look up from whatever she was reading before she was speaking.

"What the hell is this?"

"Good evening to you, too, Miss Scott."

Finally, Elena reclined in her seat, plucked her reading glasses from her nose, and studied her. That familiar amusement tugged at the corner of her lips, and it drove Maya wild.

"Seriously, Elena, I cannot accept this. That's just... crazy, and...are you trying to buy me?"

She let the check flutter down onto the table and ran a harried hand through her hair.

"And what exactly would I be purchasing?"

She was being toyed with, and today, in the face of the extremely impressive raise she had apparently received, it irked her to no end.

"Is this because of what I told you? I don't need your pity, Elena. I don't need—"

"Maya."

She sucked in a breath as she was interrupted.

"You've worked here for almost six months, you are usually the last to leave, one of the first to arrive, and can you tell me honestly you are not one of the hardest workers in that room?"

She stumbled over her response, and Elena continued.

"Your salary sans the raise is still nowhere near comparable to Dave or Kathryn, who have worked here for six and nine years respectively, but it is more in alignment with your output and the responsibilities you have taken on since starting at the foundation."

Oh.

"I apologize for the timing and for the fact that you are *utterly* unable to take a compliment, praise, or gratitude of any kind without reacting poorly, but you deserve the raise and you have earned, and I'm sure will continue to earn, every penny."

Her cheeks were scarlet, a hot flush crawled up her neck and deflated without her anger. She was humiliated that she had accused Elena of trying to buy her. Just recounting the words in her mind made her cringe.

"If you're quite finished having a tantrum, could you close the door?"

Elena's body moved in her seat, and Maya watched her, the words taking a second to register, a second for her to understand that she was being dismissed. Embarrassed beyond belief, she complied, seeing herself out and closing the door firmly at her back with a shaking hand.

She was halfway down the corridor when a very disgruntled, "Miss Scott," summoned her back. Gritting her teeth, she turned and stepped back into the office as Elena diligently held the door for her before clicking it closed behind her.

"I meant close it with you on the inside, silly girl."

Elena gave her whiplash, and her mortification died a fiery death to the spike of arousal that Elena Mars calling her a *silly girl*, of all things, had created. The lock snicked quietly into place, and she was sure she was going to combust on the spot.

Elena stepped into her space, and she was intoxicated.

"You earned the raise, Maya. Are we absolutely clear on that?"

She looked up into those bottomless brown eyes and all the care they held and nodded, resisting the urge to swallow hard as they transformed into something darker.

"Good."

Firm hands pushed her back against the door and Elena moved against her, her body bumping against Maya's at random intervals as she held her there.

"We were very rudely interrupted on Friday, and my week has been hell thinking of what I missed out on."

Elena trailed her fingers down Maya's pale cheek and ran them across her lips until Maya realized they had parted, and Elena was leaning down to kiss her.

It was soft at first, testing, and she could barely breathe.

Elena kissed her like she was something precious, something worth remembering, and the idea alone blew her mind.

When a tongue slipped warm into her mouth a soft moan left her, a match over gasoline, and the moment shattered.

"Do you have any idea how much I have wanted this, Miss Scott?"

And she didn't; she had absolutely no fucking idea, but she was ready to learn. Elena's kisses turned hard, hot, and messy, teeth and tongue and a hand roughly palming her ass against the door.

Elena was everywhere, her body jerking, her hand kneading, her tongue running slick across Maya's bottom lip and then pushing back into her mouth and claiming her, tasting her, melting her. It was all she could do to tangle her own fingers in Elena's silky ebony hair and kiss her back, panting out hot, desperate breaths into Elena's mouth.

Her hips were moving of their own accord, pushing forward against Elena, searching for a friction she could never find in their current position, and if she wasn't so consumed with her want, Maya knew she would be terrified because she had never experienced anything as explosive as this.

When Elena pulled back, she left her breathless, a panting mess against the door. She was sure her hair was a state, her lips were probably bruised, and it took all her mental faculties not to break down and beg for Elena to go on.

There was no space between them, their bodies flush together, and Maya moved as Elena moved, finding an odd sort of balance in her shaking as she waited and hoped desperately that Elena wasn't about to change her mind.

"You're beautiful."

And god, Elena was intense. She ran her fingers down the column of Maya's throat and squeezed lightly, the action unexpectedly sending her hips bucking again in a move that surprised Maya and seemed to delight Elena.

"Do you need something, Maya?"

She nodded, her head bumping against the door, her nose inches from Elena's.

She had never been one for dirty talk; it always felt too cliché, and she was always too shy, but Elena was watching her reverently, and she knew what was coming.

"What do you need, sweetheart?"

The endearment broke her. She knew she probably would have answered her anyway, but the sound of it on Elena's tongue demolished the last of her reluctance.

"You. Fuck me, Elena."

Her eyes were sheer black, her pupils blown. She pushed one hand down between their bodies and slid up the inside of Maya's trembling thigh. A soft keening sound rung in her ears as Elena pushed her panties aside, and it took Maya a few seconds to realize she was making the noise.

Elena's plump lips hissed their approval against her mouth, swallowing her next cry as surprisingly nimble fingers began working across her sensitive flesh, her body tightening way too fast.

Elena claimed every inch of her mouth, her chin, her neck. Sharp teeth were leaving a bruising indent where her throat met her shoulder when Maya finally broke, tears in her eyes and a burn between her legs unlike anything she'd ever experienced.

"Elena..."

She wanted her inside. Her body was rushing too fast, riding a wave she couldn't stop or slow down, and desperately she wanted Elena in her when it crested.

"Fuck me, please."

Elena studied her, a wicked gleam in her dark eyes, and she knew she was going to have to say it, but somehow, barreling toward what was possibly going to be the best orgasm of her life, it seemed like a small price to pay.

"Inside."

A finger entered her in response, those kiss-swollen lips returning to swallow her moan, chasing her head back as it banged against the door. One finger was followed by another, a thumb still rubbing her, and in record time Maya was losing control.

It was filthy, dirty, naughty in ways Maya had never thought she cared for, but her body proved her wrong, trembling, pitching her forward and pushing all the air out of her chest as her lips wrapped around Elena's name.

They barely stayed upright, both unsteady on their feet for different reasons. Elena stayed inside her, fucking her slowly, wringing out every drop of pleasure the moment could offer, and when she finally sagged, strong arms held her tight.

Maya had never been a crier. Winling had mentioned the "crying after a world-shattering orgasm" phenomenon a few times, but having never experienced it herself, she was totally embarrassed that, of course, Elena Mars was the one to elicit it from her for the very first time.

They stayed still, or as still as Elena was capable of, locked together against the door, two fingers still pushed deliciously inside her, soft lips kissing her cheeks and telling her she was amazing until finally, Elena stepped away.

She couldn't stop the little moan that left her as Elena's slim fingers were pulled from her skewed panties, the sound twisting into something perverse as the same fingers disappeared between Elena's lips.

Elena's eyes dared her, and she rose easily to the challenge, ready to push Elena back to perch on the edge of her desk when she caught sight of the clock.

"Oh my God. Shit... I have Livvie this weekend, and Robert will be at my place in thirty minutes."

Elena spent another long second sucking on her fingers before she removed them from her mouth and stalked forward. Maya could taste herself in the kiss.

"Go." She closed the gap between them again before she released her hold on Maya's chin.

With another quick apology and a total mess between her legs, Maya grabbed her check and rushed out of the office, resolving to pay Elena back for what was honestly the best orgasm of her life soon.

*

"Mama, where's Mm'lena, she at work?"

At this point, Maya honestly wasn't sure who was missing Elena more, her or her daughter.

"I'm not sure, Bug. It's Sunday, so she's probably at home."

Livvie was still stuck on tea parties, a large collection of Maya's mismatched kitchen mugs arranged carefully on the coffee table while they leaned back on the sofa, watching early morning cartoons, Maya periodically reminding Livvie not to pick at her cast or let the kitten scratch at it.

"Maybe she come to this home?"

She let the question hang unanswered, and mercifully, Livvie dropped it, being sucked back into the brightly colored world on the screen, scratching absently at her cast again. Swiping across her cell's screen, Maya checked her phone once more. The messages she and Elena had exchanged since Friday night had been a dizzying mix of sinful and sweet. It always warmed Maya's heart how Elena was so excited, so genuinely interested, in hearing about her time with Livvie.

She hadn't dated much since her daughter was born. Her romantic life had consisted of two poorly thought out first-date-turned-one-night-stands in the first year after she lost her, and both times, the other woman had politely steered conversation away, or flat out baulked at the mention of her child.

> *Livvie misses you. She's asking again if you can come over. You're welcome to if you wanted.*

She pressed send before she could change her mind, feeling marginally guilty about using her child as a means to fulfill her own desires, though nothing she said was technically a lie. The response came quicker than she had expected.

> *Would love to. Later this afternoon? Need me to bring dinner?*

The thrill of Elena's acceptance shot a little jolt through her chest, and Maya typed out her reply, unable to keep the smile from her face.

> *Yes, how's 3:00 p.m? No need to bring dinner. But you can if you'd like, or we can order?*

Her phone buzzed again.

> *I'll bring something. Until then, Miss Scott.*

And God, the woman could fluster her even through text message.

Resisting the urge to go and take what would have to be her fourth or fifth hot steamy shower of the weekend to relieve herself, followed by a cold one to get herself under control, she turned to Livvie instead.

"Bug, Elena just texted me, and she said she can come over later this afternoon."

The shriek of delight her daughter emitted was definitely supersonic.

*

Dinner was perfect, and Maya did not use the *P* word lightly. Elena had brought over a huge pan of lasagna, a tray of steamed vegetables, and a smaller bowl of mac and cheese in case Livvie didn't like either. She was so ridiculously thoughtful, and so patient, and Livvie absolutely adored her.

Elbow deep in the sink, washing the dishes, which Elena had valiantly fought her to do though Maya had refused, she could hear the two of them talking in the living room, their conversation punctuated by the occasional laugh.

As she was laying everything out on the drying rack, she felt eyes on her back and turned to see Elena making her way across the kitchen floor, sidestepping the cat with a pointed look, beautiful with bare feet, black leggings, and a loose long-sleeve shirt. Her fingers grazed the small of Maya's back as she moved to stand beside her.

"I hope you don't mind, but I bought something for Livvie. Would it be okay if I gave it to her now?"

She looked so unsure, so off-balance in a way that didn't feel like her at all, and eager to reassure her, Maya reached up and cradled her bobbing chin in damp hands until she dared to press a quick soft kiss to her lips, conscious of Livvie close by.

"You didn't hve to do that, but thank you, and of course you can give it to her."

Elena nodded and pulled away with a lingering look. She headed back to the front door where she had left her bag. Maya watched her go, her walk a little more unsteady than usual, and she wondered how much time she had spent preparing food for them and buying Livvie that gift and how that had affected her body.

When Maya made it back to the living room, dishes conquered, Livvie was holding a large boxed tea set in her lap, looking up at Elena with big excited eyes.

"So now you have your own tea set. This one is plastic, so it won't break, but I want you to treat it with extra special care just like the real set, okay? If you show me and your mama that you can take good care of this one, when you're a little bit bigger we'll get you a porcelain one like mine."

Maya's heart imploded. This night was something from a dream, a fairytale that just didn't happen for someone like her. The sense of permanence in the sentiment Elena shared with her daughter bowled her over, and she had to swallow the emotion gathering thick in her throat, telling herself it was stupid to *actually* pinch herself to be sure this was real.

Livvie nodded reverently, little fingers tracing the cups through the clear plastic cover of the box.

"I take goo-ood care. Love you, Mm'lena."

It wasn't a thank-you, but it was better. And it terrified Maya as much as it warmed her down to her bones. She had always been so careful to keep the few relationships she had with other adults separate from her daughter, save for Winling, so afraid to expose her to someone she would later have to miss. Her heart ached at the thought of losing Elena, for herself and for Livvie, and she hoped it would never be something they had to worry about.

"I love you, too, honey." She could hear the surprise, the thickness in Elena's voice, all the emotion there apparent even with a soft slur blanketing her words.

She watched a little while longer, a silent audience, enjoying the budding relationship between the two from her spot at the door, the confidence Elena was slowly growing, the shrill delight Livvie found in her company as they drank cup after cup of invisible tea with impeccable etiquette. Finally, she forced herself to interrupt.

"Livvie, it's bedtime."

Livvie groaned, and Elena tickled her sides until she laughed instead.

"Listen to Mama, put away your teacups, and off you go."

The little plastic cups clattered together as Elena picked them up two in each hand, Livvie reaching out to steady the shaking, giving her a killer smile Maya knew personally to be absolutely devastating.

"You come back soon?"

Elena was already nodding, played like a flute by Livvie.

"I'll check with Mama, but I'm sure we'll see each other again soon."

That seemed to be good enough for Livvie, and Maya had to press three fingers to her lips to stifle a laugh as Elena received a trademark ultraloud and slightly wet kiss on the cheek and a hug goodnight, the purple cast pressed against her neck.

With a quick glance over her shoulder she followed Livvie to her room, endlessly thankful to the powers that be when Livvie went down after only half a story, tired from the excitement of the day.

By the time she returned to the living room, the floor was clear of all the stuffed animals that had previously littered it, the cushions were straight on the sofa, and the DVD cases were all stacked neatly on the shelf.

Elena waited, a glass of the wine she had brought sloshing between her fingers, a second one sitting on the coffee table. The scene was so domestic—everything about their evening had been—and Maya's heart soared.

"You didn't have to clean up."

She was suddenly nervous as she crossed the space to sit beside Elena, though it melted easily when Elena reached out to tug her closer and kissed her gently.

"I wanted to."

"Dinner was amazing, thank you. I can't believe she ate broccoli."

Elena's shaky fingers twisted a lock of hair back behind Maya's ear before Elena leaned forward to deposit her wine on the table unsteadily.

"I cooked it with just a little garlic and removed the tough stems."

Maya nodded, though she knew she would never be able to replicate the flavor. She was an average cook on her very best day whereas Elena was amazing.

"Everything was delicious, and Livvie had the best time. The tea set was so sweet, thank you."

"No, *thank you*. Tonight was…wonderful." There was sincerity to Elena's words, a softness and a weightiness, and Maya couldn't resist leaning forward and tasting them on her lips. God, she could get used to this, real dinners and laughter filling her little home, dark eyes watching her over dinner, and Livvie's delighted chatter as Elena played enthusiastically with her. Before the thought could really take root and absolutely terrify her, Elena spoke again.

"Would you like me to leave? I completely understand. Livvie is here—"

Maya was already shaking her head, watching with curious eyes as Elena reached out to retrieve her glass, the dark-crimson liquid sloshing erratically up the side as she brought it to her lips and emptied it.

"In that case, can I take you to bed, sweetheart?"

Maya was powerless to do anything but nod, the softness of the moment stark against the dark undertone seeping into Elena's voice. Her body had ached with need almost constantly since Friday, a pleasant soreness between her legs from being full for the first time in almost two years, an experience she was desperate to repeat, though first, she wanted to touch Elena.

She quickly drained her own glass and led Elena to her room, immediately embarrassed by the worn gray comforter and pile of laundry in the corner, sure Elena's mansion was much nicer inside than her own messy apartment.

Elena was perched on the edge of her bed, her eyes a rich molten topaz in the dim light from the lamp. She was as stunning in casual clothes, hair slightly waved, makeup neutral, as she had been the night at the restaurant in a designer dress. The sight made Maya wonder how many more versions of Elena there were to discover, the thought bringing with it an aching desire to know them all.

"Come here."

She didn't have to be told twice, moving to stand between Elena's legs, bowing her head, veiling them in gold as she bent to kiss her.

Elena was a potent drug, and Maya was so easily ensnared by her. She mapped her body with careful hands, across the planes of her stomach, over the swell of her breasts, a jittering journey along the small of her back and down to her ass. Elena worked to undress her, keeping her mouth captive between each discarded article of clothing, and before she knew it, she was naked in front of her fully clothed employer. Elena must have sensed her discomfort because she kissed her stomach tenderly, not seeming to mind the small stretch marks Livvie had left behind, before she stood and discarded her own clothes with a little struggle but no hesitation. Maya watched hungrily, her breathing already haggard.

They clambered back up the mattress, laughing until their mouths met again. Elena's body was soft, an expanse of smooth skin and lean muscle that contracted at will, and Maya was lost in the feel of it against hers, naked breasts and hips and feet.

There was a softness in their exchange that wasn't there the first time, but Maya found it to be just as erotic. Elena was still slightly dominant, kissing her soundly and covering her body with her own. A shaking hand was making its way up her thigh before Maya caught herself and pushed up, flipping their position.

"I do believe, Miss Mars, that it's my turn."

Elena's dark eyes burned up at her, and God she was beautiful, dark hair splayed on her pillow and a wicked smile on her mouth.

"In that case, do what you will with me, Miss Scott."

And she did.

*

Maya tried not to smirk when Robert knocked at her door the next morning. She had rushed to answer; of course, he was fifteen minutes early, and she was still in her pajamas, something that usually would have left her mortified. Elena appeared behind her as she greeted him, already dressed in a pristine suit of slacks and blazer, dark makeup making her look formidable, and they descended into polite small talk as Maya called again for Livvie, having already passed her bag over to Holt.

She couldn't help but feel smug with Robert hovering awkwardly as Livvie kissed both her and Elena goodbye. His annoyance over the relationship was clear, as was the careful respect he showed Elena, and for once, it was so good to finally catch a glimpse of what it was like to have the upper hand. With Elena's hand soft on her waist, they waved until the elevator doors obscured Livvie from view, the sadness that usually came with watching her leave dulled by Elena's presence.

She was about to turn and begin the rush to get ready for work when Elena spoke, holding her loosely in place.

"I think it's only fair I tell you I'm not very experienced with all this."

Maya leaned back against her, still staring out into the now deserted hallway, not relishing the thought of having to move away from her. Entirely comfortable, still a little high off the wary way Robert had watched them, she didn't think too hard about Elena's declaration or her answer.

"Parenting?"

"Well... Yes, that too."

She stumbled over the words, and Maya could tell that hadn't been what she meant, *oops*. She sensed she had caught her off guard with the idea that she would be involved in Livvie's life in such a way, though somehow, she knew now that Elena wouldn't run at the implication.

"What I meant is this, you and I," she clarified carefully.

"Oh, me too."

Tipping her head, Maya looked back into Elena's eyes, their bodies rocking to the tempo of Elena's movements.

They stayed like that for a moment before reluctantly they broke apart and went back inside. Maya moved to the bedroom and rifled through her closet, getting ready for the workday, looking up from where she gave up trying to find matching socks to see Elena watching her with guarded eyes.

She was about to make a joke about her odd socks, but a seriousness in Elena's gaze stopped her. Selfishly, she didn't want it, she didn't want the argument or the issue, or whatever negative thing was coming because so far, the morning, and the previous night, had just been so good. She wanted to cling to it for a little longer, but when Elena began to speak, eyes troubled, she let the socks fall back into the hamper and listened.

"Maya, I'm fourteen years older than you, and I have CP...and honestly all my dating endeavors end horribly."

She faltered, seeming to struggle over what more to say, and Maya took her opportunity to interject.

"I don't understand what that has to do with us getting into a relationship?" She tried to keep her tone neutral, understanding, and open but firm, slightly shocked that Elena of all people was seemingly insecure about this.

"You could do so much better." The words poured out of Elena and she blushed, and Maya crossed the room in two long strides and kissed her on her silly mouth.

"Elena, you're one of the most amazing women I know. You're strong and determined and loving, my daughter adores you, we have fun together, and you make me happy. I'm excited to explore this with you."

She smoothed her fingers through Elena's thick, dark hair. A little embarrassed by her own candor but eager to assuage her fears.

"You're also absolutely crazy if you think I'm the party in this that could do better, Miss CEO, lives in a mansion, takes on the world daily."

Elena rolled her eyes and shrugged it off, a tentative smile returning slowly to her face.

"I just want you to be happy, you and Livvie."

"Then stay." The answer was that easy, and Maya also knew it was that hard.

"Are you sure?"

She nodded, letting exactly how sure she was that she wanted her shine in her eyes.

"I suppose we'll both just have to figure it out as we go then, and perhaps there is nothing better than that."

As Elena leaned down to kiss her, Maya couldn't agree more.

Chapter Eight

Dating Elena was amazing. It was lunch dates spent talking about everything, evenings listening to vinyl on her record player, walks in the park on the weekends, and taking Livvie to the science museum. It was easy and it was domestic, and Maya struggled to believe it was her life more and more, the longer she lived it.

Now, lying on a plush king-size bed in California, having flown on a plane for the first time since she was twelve and going on her first family vacation with her parents, it felt even more unreal. The sound of the water from the shower hitting the tub through the bathroom door provided an easy backdrop for her thoughts, and her mind drifted.

When Elena had asked her to come on this business trip, Maya had been unsure. It wasn't her weekend with Livvie and a weekend without Elena had seemed grim, ultimately compelling her to take the plunge and agree to go. An added bonus was that her birthday was on Saturday, something she was sure Elena didn't realize, and she was thankful for the fact. The day had become a somber affair since the death of her parents, and she was honestly glad for the distraction she knew the trip would bring, thankful for not having to spend it alone, again.

Most of the time spent together in their relationship so far had been either private with just the two of them, sometimes with Livvie, or at the office. Traveling through the airport and making the trip with Elena today had been eye-opening for Maya in a way she was still processing.

She probably should have expected some level of staring. But the whispering and the blatant pointing had caught her off guard. Elena hadn't seemed to notice, and Maya wondered how long she had been dealing with it for it to fade into the background...unless it didn't, and she had to expend the effort to ignore it every single day. She wasn't sure which made her sadder. She *was* sure she had given out more nasty looks that day than any other in her life, furious with how blatant people were in their disregard for Elena's feelings, for anything but their own selfish curiosity about her erratic movement.

When they'd arrived at the gate to check in, the attendant had asked Elena to step aside, and she'd rolled her eyes and let out a huff like she'd expected it. Maya was told to go ahead and board, but she point-blank refused to go without Elena. It was a long and embarrassing fifteen minutes sitting off to the side by the desk, watching the rest of the passengers board their plane before, finally, a supervisor appeared to ask Elena if she had been drinking and would submit to a breathalyzer in order to board.

Maya could understand it; she remembered so saliently her own confusion, her own mistake, that first day she met Elena in the bathroom in thinking she was drunk. Now she knew the truth, the incident had worked its way under her skin in a way she had struggled to hide. Logically, she could see why the pieces looked to fit—the shaking and lack of balance, the occasionally slurred speech, and the atypical gait. She could understand that the team of people there had to do their job, but she ached for Elena and for the humiliating injustice of it all.

For her part, Elena plowed through it like any other business transaction, stony-faced with a wicked sneer as she informed them she had cerebral palsy, but she would, however, agree to take the test and would appreciate if they could get the hell on with it. The only time her composure almost cracked was after the test was done and the supervisor was apologizing profusely when he offered her special seating more suitable for her *needs*.

Maya had walked ahead, content to let Elena have her conniption as she explained to him that what she *needed* was to be able to board her plane half an hour ago.

They hadn't talked about it since, and Maya had a feeling they wouldn't. Maybe it was because she was new to it in comparison to Elena, or maybe she struggled with it because she understood both sides of the coin so clearly now, but she was still mulling it all over when Elena emerged from the bathroom, one earring in her hand.

"Are you ready?"

Her hair was already styled and dried, and she had redressed in a smart-casual jeans and button-down ensemble that Maya immediately appreciated. She pushed herself up off the bed.

"I am. Need help with that?"

She gestured to the earring, watching as it was tossed down onto the beautiful hardwood vanity.

"It's a little too late for it, unfortunately. I already dropped the other one down the plughole in the sink. I know better than to try to put on earrings without putting the plug in first."

Between wondering how many pairs of earrings had suffered a similar fate and noting silently that Elena was handling this particular setback because of her CP better than usual, Maya donned her leather jacket.

"Are you going to tell me where we're going yet?"

Elena struggled with her coat, finally slipping into it, and moved on to wrestling the oversized buttons closed.

"Business, unfortunately. One of the TMF beneficiary charities has been having a difficult time recently. I have a check to take to them and thought a visit may help morale, let them know they haven't been forgotten, that people do care."

Though her tone was all business, Elena's big heart shone through, and again Maya wondered how the people around her didn't see this woman for everything she was beneath her abrasive front, so generous and thoughtful and brimming with compassion.

"That sounds amazing, lead the way."

Having never been to California, the cab ride to the charity was an event in itself. They rode in content silence, their hands linked, bouncing lightly on the seat between them with the movement of Elena's body. Maya studied the city as it passed by outside the window, similar to New York in some ways and glaringly different in others.

The pace of life seemed slower here, the people looked brighter somehow, and she hoped they would have a little time to immerse themselves in that, though the ordeal at the airport still hung over her. She wasn't ashamed of Elena, far from it, but her chest ached for her every time someone whispered a little too loud or stared a little too long.

"Maya."

She jumped.

Elena was counting out bills with some difficulty. She dropped them into the front seat, earning her a glare from the cab driver which made Maya wish she could explain to him that it probably wasn't intentional. For her part, Elena just seemed uncaring about the whole thing.

"Ready to go?"

They climbed out of the cab, Elena's hand reaching out to grasp Maya's so she could steady herself, and then they were standing on the sidewalk and it was dawning on Maya that somewhere amidst her thoughts, they had left the nicer part of town.

"This is where the charity is?"

Elena gave her hand what felt like a reassuring shake before she let it drop.

"Yes, it's right over here, according to the map application."

They trudged forward, and even with the late afternoon sun warm on her back, Maya couldn't shake the unease settling over her. She was no stranger to this kind of neighborhood but being back in such a rundown area with Elena made her nervous.

"We're here."

When Elena stopped in front of a sign proclaiming the large house before them to be the Sunnyvale Children's Home, everything aligned for Maya.

"I understand if you don't want to come inside. I just thought you might like to see the impact of some of your hard work at TMF firsthand."

Wiping her sweating palms on her jeans, Maya nodded. She wasn't that girl anymore; she had come so far, grown so much, and she could do this, or at least that's what she told herself.

"That would be nice."

Elena must have sensed her hesitance, reaching up with a jerky hand to squeeze her arm loosely before she led her to the door and struggled with the bell.

Being led inside the home was a blast from the past Maya wasn't ready for: the noise of too many voices, the sparse and impersonal furniture, the double row of coat hangers each with a name written on a piece of tape below. The social worker led them through and introduced them to the director, and feeling suddenly small, Maya was glad when Elena took the lead easily, introducing them in return and thanking her for scheduling the visit. She smiled half-heartedly and shook the woman's hand.

Their meeting passed in somewhat of a blur, Elena and the director discussing allocation of funds and improvement of the facilities, leaving Maya alone with her thoughts for the most part.

"If it's all right, I'd like to meet with the children, hear their thoughts, and get some ideas for new material for your section of our webpage. Maybe we can come up with a list of the most urgent requirements that we can focus on obtaining funding for?"

Elena like this always surprised her. Maya could tell from the introductions that this was her first time meeting the Sunnyvale director, but she had wasted no time in getting right down to business, and thankfully her ever-changing posture and the coarse tremor in her hands hadn't been an issue at all.

"Of course, I think they would enjoy having a chance to voice their opinions. They have plenty, trust me."

They shared a laugh, and Maya forced herself to join in, trying to pull herself out of the introspective trance falling over her, as they were led to what seemed to be the dining room, doubling as a meeting hall.

Extra chairs were pulled up and bodies filed in. They sat at the head of the table, watching teenager after teenager taking their place. Boys and girls of different ethnicities and obviously differing ages. Maya tried not to look too closely, terrified to see anything she recognized in any of them—anything to remind her of herself and the time after her parents died when this was her life too.

"Are you doing all right?"

Even barely above a whisper, the concern in Elena's voice was evident.

"I'm fine, it's just...a blast from the past, y'know?"

Elena nodded.

"Everyone, this is Elena and her colleague, Maya. They work at The Mars Foundation and are responsible for the new furniture we got last year, among other things. They'd like to talk to you today about continuing to improve the house. If you could all give them your attention, and your *polite* thoughts, that would be appreciated."

The director stepped back, and Elena cleared her throat.

"Hello, everyone. Before anyone asks, I'm not drunk."

A snicker rose in the room, and slowly, pairs of disinterested eyes began to focus.

"Though it wouldn't be the first time on this trip, or in my life, someone has thought so. I would say I'm just so excited to be here, but really, I have cerebral palsy, so forgive my inability to sit still."

And just like that, she had connected with them. Maya wondered what made it so much easier for her to be open with children, thinking back to her honest explanation of her disability to Livvie, too, and comparing it to her own experience as an adult, when she first met Elena.

As the discussion wore on, she began to enjoy herself, discomfort morphing into catharsis, as more and more she realized that they really had impacted these kids through TMF, and they would continue to do so.

"So, what do you guys still need?"

They had established a system of raising hands to speak after the answers to their initial questions had devolved into a shouting match. Half a dozen hands shot up, and Elena indicated to each of them when it was their turn to speak.

"The new PlayStation."

"A new washing machine. Ours makes the clothes smell weird."

"A library."

"Flat-screen TVs."

"New pillows."

The answers were varied: some funny, some extravagant, and some a little sad. Elena navigated them all with grace and by the time the meeting was concluded, Maya was smiling. At first it was painful, uncomfortably familiar being at the home, but the more she realized she had the power to help, the more she could somehow acknowledge the change in her own life and how far she had come.

The cab ride back to the hotel was quiet, Elena speaking only to ask her if she'd prefer to go out or dine in the room, seeming to sense her need to be alone with her thoughts. It wasn't unpleasant, but a new awareness definitely hung around her and she felt further now than she ever had from the rocky shores of her past, and the troubles of her nineteen-year-old self.

With the door to their room finally closed behind them, Maya released a long-held breath, making an effort to shake off her introspection and enjoy what was left of their evening.

"Are you all right, sweetheart?"

Elena's touch was tentative on her hip as she came to stand behind her at the bar in the kitchen. Relieved to feel her touch, Maya leaned back into her ever-moving body.

"I'm fine, that was kind of nice."

"If it was too much... I just thought—" There was an apology in her voice.

"Elena." Maya turned in her arms and kissed her softly. "It was good, I needed it, thank you."

Relief shone in Elena's eyes.

"You're sure?"

She nodded.

"Okay then." They kissed again and Maya felt herself coming back into the moment, and with Elena's grip loose on her waist and her tongue ghosting her lips, it was a beautiful place to be.

"We should eat." She interrupted despite herself, a little worried by the number of miles they had covered today, plus their long visit to the home and what it would mean for Elena's health. Her tremor had steadily worsened as they travelled, her body bumping softly against Maya's as they stood together by the counter.

"I was planning on it."

Elena gave her a wicked grin, and she rolled her eyes.

"Were you planning to order takeout or...?"

With one last smoldering look, Elena let her go. She moved to the door and produced a thin laminated card. She took a seat on the sofa and patted the spot beside her.

Studying the card, Maya settled down into the plush suede. "Room service? When I said I would rather eat here, I didn't mean we had to do that. I mean, wow, look at the prices."

Elena waved her off and she tried not to baulk at how little ordering a fifty-dollar plate seemed to bother her.

"It's all part of the budget. Besides, tomorrow is an important day. I think you deserve a treat tonight."

Her voice was wicked, sinful, but Maya could barely appreciate it, still reeling with the fact that somehow, Elena knew it was her birthday. Thinking it over, she guessed it was in her personnel file. Perhaps she got a reminder for all the staff birthdays?

"Tomorrow?" she questioned, not wanting to be incorrect in her assumption.

"Do you want the steak, darling?"

She nodded, impressed again that Elena had learned her preference for food and her love for a good steak, as well as so much else about her, so quickly.

"Medium? Steamed veggies okay?"

She agreed to both, watching Elena use the voice dial on her phone to call the number on the card and order their dinner before she turned back to her.

"Are you one of those people who doesn't like to celebrate their birthday? If it's an age thing, you'll only be twenty-three and that's far too young to worry about that."

Maya rolled her eyes playfully before she felt herself grow somber.

"I just—" She struggled to explain it, especially with their visit to the home still so fresh. "For the first fifteen years of my life I had these wonderful birthdays, and my sixteenth, the first one without my parents, and all the ones since, they just became another glaring reminder."

Elena's hand covered hers, squeezing it gently, her dark eyes filled with patience and understanding.

"Once the rawness of losing them started to heal there was Livvie, and the loneliness that comes with spending my birthdays without her. I've not had the good luck to have it fall on my weekend with her yet." She trailed off, embarrassed about bringing so much doom and gloom to their trip.

"My birthdays were never all that fantastic either. In boarding school, it was just another day, and the times I was home Mother was usually busy with her own things. My father would try. He always sent me a beautiful card, and his gifts were small but meaningful, little things I treasured. Looking back, I wish I'd been brave enough to tell him what I treasured the most was his company... But of course, he just did what Mother wanted, so I'm not sure it would have mattered anyway."

She sighed, and once again Maya felt a connection, the feeling of loneliness that usually followed her dissolving. Even Winling, who knew her better than almost anybody in the world, struggled to relate to her sometimes, having a large and close and periodically overbearing family who were never far away.

"What about your adult birthdays?"

Maya couldn't help but be curious.

"They were okay for a while, but as the years passed, they became something I came to dread rather than celebrate—another year older, another year without really finding anyone, another year too late for a family."

She instantly felt guilty.

"Elena."

"It's fine, darling, really. I've made my peace with it."

Even Maya could sense the lie in her words.

"We don't have to celebrate your birthday tomorrow if you don't want to, but I would like to spoil you anyway. Seems I have you all to myself until our flight in the evening."

She was deflecting the conversation away from herself, but Maya decided to allow it, ready to answer when they were interrupted by a knock at the door.

The food arrived on honest to God silver platters, and having never ordered room service in her life, Maya was somehow embarrassed when the perfectly cooked steak was uncovered and set down before her on the coffee table, the water she asked for poured into a misty iced glass. Again, this just didn't feel like her life.

They ate in a companionable silence, though it grew harder to concentrate thanks to the thorough eye-fucking Elena was giving her over her salad. She made a valiant effort, cutting her food into tiny pieces and trying to ignore the eyes that seemed to roam over her face, her neck, her body, wondering if this was going to happen every time they ate. She was just about to try to make a joke that Elena should order something other than salad and maybe she would be more interested in her food and less in looking at her like *that*, but the minute she looked up at her the words died on her lips. Finally giving up, Maya pushed her plate away.

"Mind if I put this in the fridge? I hate to waste it. I can probably finish it tomorrow."

"Would you take mine too?"

She nodded and took Elena's plate, admittedly spending a little longer than was strictly necessary bent over moving the plates around on the shelf, giving Elena what she hoped was a clear view of her backside.

When she straightened up, her eyes were almost black.

"Would you care for a nightcap on the balcony, Miss Scott?"

That was the very last thing Maya had been expecting to hear, but she nodded anyway, knowing when Elena was looking at her like that, she would care for pretty much anything she had to offer.

She followed her out into the still warm air, moving to the railing, the city lights of Los Angeles beautiful against the backdrop of the stars.

"Absolutely breathtaking."

She turned at the sound of Elena's voice, surprised to find Elena not looking out at the skyline but studying her face intensely instead. Her tongue slid over her lips on instinct, dampening them for the kiss she ached for. It never came. Instead, a half full small glass of clear liquor was pressed into her hand.

"Drink up."

The tequila slid down her throat as she wondered absently if Elena had spilled half of it on the way over to her, or only filled the glass halfway to avoid such a thing to begin with.

When her eyes opened after squeezing shut as the taste overpowered her, they were met with the sight of Elena sucking a lime wedge between her lips. Maya could taste it on her tongue as Elena leaned in to kiss her, pushing easily into her mouth.

"I've waited all day to do this, Miss Scott."

"Do what?" She was already breathless, anticipation beating a heady drum in her veins, as Elena took their glasses and set them on the small patio table. Maya almost followed before she was pushed back against the railing.

"Whatever you want me to, darling."

Shaky hands were already moving up her thighs, up over her hip and down to palm her backside, and Maya's tongue darted out to wet her lips again.

"Kiss me."

Elena did, thoroughly, all lips and teeth and tongue, rough kisses that made Maya's heart race and her underwear damp.

By the time they pulled apart, careful fingers were rubbing her through her jeans, her hips moving lightly with their rhythm.

"Should we go inside?" Her voice was lower, thick, already heavy with her want, but somehow, she wasn't as embarrassed as she would once have been, safe in Elena's embrace.

"Why?" Elena's voice was wicked, and Maya knew there was a game afoot.

"Because I want you."

A soft kiss rewarded her words, Elena watching her intently.

"What exactly do you want, Maya?"

She would never get tired of hearing her name in that voice, the syllables drawn out over hot coals that made her body burn.

"I want you."

A single finger traced her lips messily thanks to the jerking of Elena's hand before it pulled her bottom lip down, opening her mouth just slightly.

"Be specific."

It wasn't a request, and the command made Maya's breath catch.

"Fuck me, Elena."

A thigh slipped between hers, Elena's hand catching the railing at her waist for a second until she had steadied herself on her feet.

"I intend to, darling, but I don't want to do it inside."

Oh.

Maya's heart rate soared as Elena's plump lips brushed her ear and that thigh exerted delicious pressure where she needed it the most.

"I want to fuck you right here against this railing." Elena ground hard against her. "Would that be all right?"

Her answer was lost on a moan, head back, hair flying loose over the balcony as Elena's painted red lips pressed against her exposed throat.

"Happy birthday, my love." Her voice was fire and ice and quite possibly the sexiest thing Maya had ever heard. "Unbutton your pants for me, sweetheart."

Chapter Nine

For the first time, work at TMF was hell. A huge online campaign they had been running for three months was drawing to a close, leaving in its wake thousands of donations to be allocated. The same number of donors had to be thanked and listed on the webpage, benefactor charities needed to be announced, and the press coverage organized. It was a logistical giant on top of their day-to-day duties.

Maya worked hard, harder than she could ever remember working for anything, and it felt good. As much as she missed the quiet of their weekend getaway, the thrill of waking up with Elena and having her full attention for an entire three days, the experience at the children's home they had visited made her work all the more worth it.

Elena's birthday gift to her was a beautiful diamond pendant given to her at dinner in a quaint little restaurant overlooking the ocean. It was probably one of the most expensive things Maya now owned, but somehow it didn't make her feel bought in a way it once might have. It made her feel cherished.

Her life was full like she had never dared to dream it might be—an amazing job that mattered, a woman like Elena, and the increasingly steely determination that she was ready to fight Robert and win, growing every day.

Elena had been working harder than anyone, the first to arrive and the last to leave by many hours, if the text messages Maya received when she was lying in bed and Elena was leaving the office were anything to go by. Their relationship—it still gave her a little thrill to be able to think of it like that—had consisted of quick kisses and long text messages and not much else for the last few days as the fundraiser wound down into a huge pile of work.

Today was one of the rare days Elena was working in the main office with them all, the team needing to attack their tasks as a unit, working together and filling in for one another with their boss at the helm. For Maya, it was making for a very unproductive Thursday.

She tried to work quickly, to be efficient, but it was utterly distracting. Elena using *that* tone of voice, the little furrow in her brow when she was deep in concentration, the accidental jerk which sent a cup of pens flying conveniently into Kevin's lap. She was beautiful, and Maya marveled that, somehow, Elena wanted *her*.

It was approaching lunch by the time she finally hit her rhythm, though her eyes were never far from Elena, worried by her increasingly sloppy speech, and the pen she was having so much trouble controlling. She watched from behind her hair as Elena grabbed her right arm with her left, trying to steady its shaking enough to sign something vaguely resembling her name on the paper Margaret patiently held flat for her. She had already torn through two copies, which had to be reprinted. Maya had never seen her symptoms this severe, and she was sure she was overworking herself.

Knowing Elena would take such an observation about as well as a house fire, she grit her teeth and let it go for now, resolving to try to talk to her that evening if they got some time alone at the end of the day.

Her fingers were moving fast over the keys, hundreds of names and places, the office buzzing around her at a steady hum. She was sinking back into her work, buoyed and carried along by the quiet concentration swelling around her, when a loud thud silenced it completely.

Whipping around in her seat, she saw Elena on the floor, one shoe lost, the split of her skirt folded embarrassingly high where she landed. To Maya's horror she was lying there, flapping against the ground as her arms didn't seem to have the strength to push her back up to sit and then stand.

She moved and it seemed to break the rest of the room from its stunned silence. Margaret was beside her in a second, and together they rolled Elena onto her back and pulled her into a sitting position. Elena's eyes were glassy and burning with a fury that terrified Maya slightly and reminded her of their first meeting.

Elena batted them away, insisting she could take it from there. Watching her as she fixed her hair and chased a jerking foot with a shaky hand to replace her shoe with every eye in the office fixed on her, Maya was reminded again that she was the strongest woman she knew.

Her heart broke as Elena tried to get up, twice, landing with another heavy thud on her bottom as she failed. She wanted to turn on all her coworkers and yell for them to give her some privacy, to have some fucking humility for God's sake. Instead, they continued to stare while Elena had to concede to allow herself to be hoisted back to her feet by the two women at her side.

As soon as she was up, she was scrambling away, her gait more off balance than Maya had ever seen it, her feet too far apart as she staggered to her own office without saying a word.

Kevin scoffed behind her, and the blood rushed to the muscles in Maya's left arm as she readied herself to turn around and deck him. Her anger at the communal shock and lack of action she had just experienced combined with the embarrassment she felt for Elena, the hurt she knew she would be feeling over this, made her temper for Kevin's crap dangerously short.

Mercifully, Margaret got there first, and he was backing up, flopping into his seat, and looking up shame-faced at the little woman who was uncharacteristically fierce, her hands on her hips as she chastised him.

The office was slowly stirring back to life, and Maya took the moment of distraction to slip away and take off after Elena. She knew someone was bound to notice, and so the whole office would know by proxy, but at that point in time, she didn't care. She was being a decent human being; if they read anything into it beyond that, it wasn't her fault. She and Elena had talked briefly and decided to keep their relationship out of the office, though Elena insisted she was the boss and she could date whoever she wanted; it just seemed less complicated, for now.

Her office door was closed.

Maya knocked once and then again when she received no response. Alight with fear that Elena had fallen again, she tried the handle only to find it was locked.

"Elena... It's me."

Silence was her response.

"Let me in, please. I'm worried about you."

Again, nothing.

"Elena, please don't make me break down your office door and cause a scene."

She heard a shuffling from inside and then the lock clicked. When the door didn't open, she stepped forward and pushed down the handle slowly, opening it just enough so she could slip inside and close it behind her.

Elena had been crying. Her eyes were red-rimmed and ever so slightly swollen, and Maya ached for her. She was about to go to her, but Elena was faster.

"I don't need your pity, or your help, Miss Scott. I'm quite fine, and I believe you have a job to do right now."

The ice in her voice caught Maya off guard, planting doubt in her chest, but the tear tracks on Elena's cheeks gave her the strength to overcome it. Slowly, she made her way across the space, and Elena looked livid at the intrusion.

"I know you're hurting." She held her hands up. "I understand if you want to be alone, I just need to know you're okay. I...I care about you, Elena, and I'm sorry if that makes you angry, but I'm scared. This is new for me and I need to know you're physically all right."

She tried to be honest without further damaging Elena's already dented pride. It seemed to work. The fire in Elena's eyes extinguished, and she looked small again, barely staying upright on her bare feet where Maya guessed she had kicked off her shoes. She looked as if she might cry, again, and Maya realized she was not prepared. She was horrible with crying people, even her own kid. She never knew what to do, always stumbling over how to react, knowing she herself hated pity.

"Can I hold you?"

It was the only thing she could think to say, and the only thing she wanted.

Elena's brown eyes were filled with tears when she nodded, and Maya rushed forward and wrapped her arms around her as Elena's breathing broke into an erratic rhythm that told Maya she was crying. She held on tight.

The shaking of the sobs and the jerking of her body left Elena feeling fragile in Maya's grasp, a too-small form being tossed around by her own forces. Maya clung to her and steadied her as much as she could, kissing dark hair and wishing she knew what to say, wishing she could erase what had just happened.

When the sobs finally subsided, Elena avoided her eyes as she scrubbed at her face with an honest to God cotton handkerchief. At any other time, the knowledge Elena possessed such a handkerchief would have made Maya laugh out loud. Watching her dab at her slightly smudged makeup, all she wanted was to get her out of there.

"Let me take you home, baby?"

It was a foul tactic and she knew it. She looked up at Elena through thick dark lashes, letting her voice turn soft and loving, as she hoped her own puppy dog eyes worked as well as her daughter's had on Elena.

Surprisingly, Elena didn't fight; she simply nodded. That troubled Maya most of all.

*

She had worried how they would explain it, what they might say to Margaret, but Elena didn't seem to care. They had left the office without a word, both keeping their heads down and moving as quickly as they could through the shared space, calling the elevator without looking back at the silence that had fallen over the office with their arrival and impending departure.

Elena informed her as they drove home in Maya's Mustang that she would text Margaret and take care of it, and she did. It had never really occurred to Maya how difficult small daily tasks could be for her girlfriend; she was so untouchable somehow. She owned everything she set her hand to with a raw power, an effortlessness, that had all the eyes on her gliding over her challenges and seeing only her success. As Maya listened to her dictate the message to her phone, she wondered how much more she had left to learn about Elena, how much she fought for everyday things that were so easy to take for granted.

The drive home had been quiet, Elena's head lolling against the window, her dark eyes defeated, falling closed occasionally until a bump in the road opened them again. Maya was led through the house, having to catch Elena around the waist twice as she stumbled. Elena had been in the bathroom for the better part of twenty minutes now, and Maya wondered if she should be concerned.

Perched on the edge of a decadent king-size bed, Maya tried to will away the annoying smattering of nerves that were making a home in her chest. The mansion was, in reality, a gorgeous detached house in a very wealthy suburb of the city and something Maya had only dreamed of and never actually experienced in person. Elena had nonchalantly informed her there were five bedrooms when she'd asked, not noticing the anxiousness coloring her voice as the different worlds they hailed from were cast into stark relief against those perfect, white walls.

The time alone, waiting on the end of the bed, feeling absolutely out of place in Elena's gorgeously opulent bedroom, made her realize her life was leading her down a path she did not want to go. It was hard enough to believe someone like Elena would choose to be with someone like her without bearing witness to their extreme wealth difference firsthand.

"Sorry I kept you waiting."

She looked small coming out of the bathroom, weary. Sweats clinging to her frame, her face free of makeup, fluffy socks dragging the carpet as she walked. She tossed a bundle of soft clothes to Maya and moved to the bed. She was a million miles from the omnipotent Elena at the office in that moment, but Maya's heart swelled because she was just as beautiful.

She slipped under the covers, the dark eyes that found Maya's still hardened, defenses back in place after the embarrassment of the day, though she wasn't totally shutting her out. Deciding to give her a little more time, Maya took the bundle of clothes and disappeared into the bathroom. She changed slowly, swinging between worrying about Elena's physical health and about her own comparative lack of wealth.

Her stomach began to ache from the stress, and she checked her appearance once more in the mirror above the sink, her eyes vividly green in the light, her curls present but drooping slightly since she had seen them this morning. Leaving her work clothes on top of a cabinet, she headed back into the room and perched on the edge of the bed. Elena watched her with tired eyes.

"I suppose you have questions?"

Maya had never felt more like a burden, and the feeling must have shown on her face because with a heavy sigh, Elena backtracked.

"Forgive me, sweetheart. I'm just...not used to being around anyone when I feel like this." She opened her arms, and Maya went willingly, slipping under the heavy comforter and leaning against plush pillows, close enough to touch but far enough away that she could still see Elena's face as she spoke.

"How do you feel?"

For a few long seconds there was no reply. She watched Elena's plump lips begin to speak once, twice, before she seemed to change her mind on what to say, until finally, she answered.

"Tired, weak. Humiliated."

The last word was quieter, and Maya found Elena's cold hand under the covers and squeezed it in her own.

"What happened? I mean, are you just working too hard or...are you sick?" She swallowed down the fear the last suggestion brought.

"Unfortunately, this is just another part of my CP." Elena said the term like it was dirty, and Maya thought she had never seen more disdain in those dark eyes than she did in that moment. "I apologize if I misled you, I do function well most of the time, but there are still days, and they can be frequent, where I just—"

"Struggle?" Maya supplied the word and she nodded.

"We all have bad days, and you haven't misled me at all. I don't know enough about this, about you, but I want to. I want to help you and be able to support you, and that means I have to understand what's going on with you."

Elena's eyes were boring into hers and she hoped she hadn't said something wrong. None of it was coming out quite like she meant it, but she had to get her point across.

"I know you don't like to talk about it or make a big deal over it, and it's not, it's totally not a big deal, but it is a part of your life, and I want to be a part of your life too. So, if this is something that can happen, I need to know what it means and how I can help."

Suddenly braver, she reached up to brush a lock of Elena's hair back behind a shaking shoulder.

"I did try to do some reading but obviously it wasn't enough—"

Elena was staring at her, looking awestruck, and she was convinced she had said something horribly dumb or accidentally offensive.

"You tried to learn about CP, for me?"

She said it like Maya had performed some monumental feat on her behalf.

"Of course, I did. I didn't want to pry in things you weren't ready to share, but I wanted to understand, to know more about you and what you need. After that night in your car when you showed me the modifications, I realized that thousands of people live with this, and other"—she stopped herself from saying disabilities, unsure how Elena would react—"other issues, and I have absolutely no idea about any of it. I want to do better than that because it's important."

Elena leaned across the space between them and kissed her hard, a ghost of the Elena who had fucked her against her office door, teased her in the bathroom, devoured her on her bed, back for just a moment before she flopped against her pillows again. They were quiet for a long moment before Elena began to speak softly.

"I have ataxic CP, so you were confused because there are three types. Mine is the least common and least talked about and the other two probably didn't sound much like me at all."

Maya nodded but didn't speak, giving Elena the opportunity to go on instead.

"When I was born the umbilical cord wrapped around my neck, starving me of oxygen and damaging the part of my brain responsible for movement, among other things. You've noticed the shaking, the tremors, difficulty to perform fine movements such as writing. I struggle with balance and coordination basically."

She paused to swallow hard and Maya raised their joined hands and kissed the tan knuckles that bumped against her lips, as she waited for her to continue.

"Less obvious are the speech issues. I was lucky to get so much therapy for that, but intonation can be hard for me. When I'm tired you may notice I start to speak in more of a monotone and the words become slurred, and in addition to the shaking is the muscle weakness. Some days it causes me to fall, as you saw. Sometimes the balance issues can do the same."

She trailed off and Maya scooted closer, wrapped her arms around her and held her tight, knowing how incredibly difficult this conversation must be for her, understanding that every word cost her.

"I do take medication to help with the tremors, and I do yoga religiously to improve my balance and core strength."

Maya hummed appreciatively against the soft skin of Elena's neck, trying to lighten the moment.

"That explains a lot, and I have to say I approve of the yoga."

Elena scoffed.

"I have to keep up with you somehow, don't I?"

Maya shrugged, a smile tugging at her mouth. Elena was letting her in, and she felt so privileged, so lucky that she was sharing this with her, that Elena had deemed her worthy of knowing her beyond the walls.

"I'm really very lucky. My CP is only mild to moderate at best, and I've had so many opportunities to learn to live with it. I'm able to walk, and drive, and speak relatively well."

"But on a day like today, how do I help you?"

Elena considered it for a moment.

"I should have known better than to come to work today. I've been feeling out of it since last night, and I had a feeling today might be a tough day but we had so much to do... Usually I just need to rest, increase my meds, and hope it calms down before I fall flat on my face in front of my entire staff."

The edge of humor was creeping into her tone, and Maya was relieved that Elena seemed to be beginning to move past the incident from earlier.

"So, you're telling me that I order you back to bed and keep you company all day?"

A perfectly sculpted eyebrow rose in challenge and, using the voice that had ruined far too many pairs of Maya's underwear to count, Elena conceded, "You can try."

And then her mouth was on Maya's. They kissed for a few minutes, gentle lips morphing into open mouths, and even in their kisses Maya noticed Elena seemed unsteady, her mouth clumsier, the press of fingers around her hips weaker than usual. When Elena ran the tip of her tongue messily across the edge of her teeth, Maya forced herself to pull back, breathless.

"I think you're supposed to be resting, baby."

"I suppose you're right." And God, Elena's voice was rough and thick and dark in a way that made Maya want her to split her open and swallow her whole. Her breath caught in her throat and Elena snickered softly at the sound, making no move to stop what they were doing.

Elena ran her smooth palm ran across the flat expanse of Maya's pale stomach, pushing up the T-shirt until she was kneading Maya's small breasts through the thin fabric of her bra, her mouth hot on the column of Maya's slender neck.

Locking down her arousal and reminding herself Elena was sick, Maya forced herself to put a stop to things before she lost the ability, the willpower, to do so.

"Elena...unghh..."

She was cupping her through her underwear, rubbing her hard enough that Maya's hips were bucking in time, the friction she was receiving too much and nowhere near enough.

"You need to rest."

She panted out the words like she had just run a marathon, relieved and frustrated beyond belief when the pressure between her legs ceased.

When she forced her eyes open, Elena's dark ones were on her, dancing with amusement, and even makeup-less and exhausted, Elena made her ache.

"Tease."

She grumbled the word as she rolled onto her side facing away from Elena, pouting half in a joke and half for real, her stomach wound tight, her thighs clenching uselessly together, trying to find the relief she had been chasing. Elena's hold over her body was ridiculous. She had never been an overly sexual person, but something about the way she touched her, the way she looked at her, whatever claiming thing lived in her kiss, made Maya whole and left her completely undone and wanting.

"Just giving myself something to look forward to when I wake up from my nap, sweetheart."

Elena's lips were perversely close to her ear, her breath hot over sensitive flesh, and Maya shuddered at the words.

"You're evil."

"Perhaps. They say absolute power corrupts and making you squirm makes me feel oh so powerful, Miss Scott. If that makes me evil, I accept the title gladly."

Her voice was dark chocolate and black coffee and sex, and Maya slapped at the arm around her waist lightly.

"Please shut up or you're going to wake up to a very grumpy me after a cold shower."

Her laugh was soft and smoky in response and she pulled Maya closer.

Content silence hung around them for several long minutes, and just as she was wondering if Elena was sleeping, she spoke again.

"I've been meaning to find a moment to ask you. Did you decide whether you're going to file for custody of Livvie?"

The question caught Maya off guard, though for the first time, she wasn't absolutely terrified by it, finally resolute in her decision.

"I did decide."

Elena hummed her approval, her body bumping against Maya's as she turned on the mattress and made herself comfortable pressed up against her back.

"And?"

Closing her eyes again and relishing the arm slung securely around her waist, the weight of Elena's body at her back, Maya let her answer fall out without letting it drag her down into the turmoil that had plagued her for so long. Finally, she was confident she could do this.

"I am."

Chapter Ten

After Elena's fall Maya had worried endlessly about her, and spent a lot more time reading about Ataxic CP. Since the day Elena had talked about her condition with her, their relationship had palpably evolved. Less and less she got the abrasive Elena, the overly sexual side of Elena, the Elena who would do anything to keep the focus away from her own challenges. Maya cherished the new level of honesty between them, a vulnerability that was somehow fostering the trait in herself too. They talked about everything, her fears deep down that Livvie was having a better life with Robert, her fear that her court case would fall flat.

Elena was constant, steady in a way Maya hadn't known in so long, between group homes and an unplanned pregnancy and then jumping from job to job and never quite landing on her feet. She was long nights spent at the mansion or her apartment, tan fingers around Maya's throat and her name on her lips as their bodies twisted in the sheets like her fingers in Elena's ebony hair. She was quiet Sunday mornings and jerking hands that spilled three cups of coffee. She was ingraining herself into Maya's life, conquering the walls that usually held her safe, and bringing with her a new era that Maya knew she was falling in love with.

She clicked away at her keyboard, glad that five o'clock had already gone and she was almost at the end of the workday. Elena stormed toward her, arriving back from the meeting that had claimed most of her day, murder in her eyes.

"Miss Scott, could you join me in my office?"

The words were a rumbling hiss, and Maya's stomach sank. Dating the boss or not, she still struggled to feel secure in her job, to stop holding her breath and waiting for the rug to be ripped out from under her feet again.

Margaret gave her a confused look, and she shrugged in response, glad that only the supervisor and Kathryn were left in the office to bear witness to this curt exchange.

The day after Elena's fall, she was hailed as a hero for rushing to her aid and offering to drive her home, no one any the wiser to the truth of their relationship. It irked Maya that they treated Elena like a pariah, but unable to word things in any other way, she took the excuse they provided for her absence and let the subject drop reluctantly.

"Miss Scott."

Shit, Elena was mad, and thankfully steadier on her feet of late. Maya pushed up from her desk and followed obediently, wondering if the little spike of adrenaline in her blood, slightly pleasurable against the backdrop of her worry, meant she enjoyed the powerful side of Elena a little too much.

Sensing the weight of what was coming, she stepped into the office and closed the door behind her.

"Do you think I'm some kind of invalid?"

That, she was not expecting.

"What the hell, Elena, of course not."

"Then what? Are you trying to embarrass me?" She was hissing mad, and Maya hovered by the chair she usually sat in, deciding to stand and stay on a level with her.

"Do you have any idea what it takes for someone like me to succeed in a position like this? A woman, Latina, lesbian, physically challenged."

Confusion washed over her. Why was she suddenly the enemy?

"Baby—"

"Don't you dare." Elena was livid, her eyes blazing infernos, her lips twisted into a sneer that Maya hadn't seen in so long. "Let me tell you about my day, Miss Scott. I'm sure you'll recall the meeting Margaret had you reschedule for me."

Her heart plummeted into her stomach as, finally, she had an inkling of what had gone wrong.

"I arrived today, at a very male-dominated company mind you, to be greeted by one of the few female employees on the front desk. I was informed that my meeting had been moved to the ground floor to better accommodate me." She spat the words out. Maya opened her mouth to speak but Elena was quicker. "The group of white, middle-aged men I was meeting with arrived, and gallantly showed me the disabled restroom they thought would suit my needs, and seated me closest to it and told me to go ahead and use it any time I needed to. I am *not* incontinent." Fury blazed on her face. "I am not incapable of using an elevator or climbing stairs, I do not need to be catered to, and in this case looked down on because of it. I don't need my peers falling asleep during the poor *disabled* girl's presentation. And I do not need you going behind my back and *preparing* people to deal with me."

She was shaking, rocking so hard her knuckles bumped against the desk creating an offbeat knocking sound that she didn't even seem to notice.

"I don't want your sympathy, Maya, I told you that from the very start, and if that's how you see me, some pet project, someone to pity, then there's no future for us."

Her voice had slipped into a monotone, cold and unfeeling, and Maya forced away the panic it sent spilling into her chest. Perhaps she had made a mistake, but she was not the one this anger should be directed toward.

"Elena, I arranged that meeting right after you fell. They asked me if there were any special considerations, and I didn't know what to say, so I mentioned you had some balance issues."

"I do not!" she roared, the last word distorted as her mouth refused to fully cooperate. "You do not speak for me or assume to know what I can and cannot do. Not as my employee, and not as someone who had an important place in my life."

The past tense hit Maya like a ton of bricks, but Elena was a woman worth fighting for, so where she would usually turn and run, she stood and fought.

"I understand that you're upset, and I am sorry I embarrassed you, but you are acting like I did it maliciously. I did the wrong thing for the right reason, Elena. I was worried about you."

"I do not need your pity."

"It's not pity to be concerned for your wellbeing, to want to know you're okay, and to want life to treat you kindly, because I love you and you're always fighting uphill. Just because I wanted for your life to be easier *for once*, does not mean I pity you."

It took three seconds after she had finished half-yelling and a long inhale before she realized she had said she loved her.

The words hung between them and Maya felt tears prick the back of her eyes as she searched Elena's hard ones for any sign of understanding, anything she could recognize in the woman who had somehow worked her way inside her to the point it was physically painful, a white-hot hole burning in her chest, in the face of losing her.

"Get out."

The hole tripled in size, tearing her apart, hot tears on her cheeks as she turned and yanked open the door. She power-walked to the staircase, unwilling to wait for the elevator or go back for her bag, desperate just to disappear.

*

It had taken Winling the best part of two hours to finally get Maya to talk about it. They'd appeared at her door half an hour after a teary phone call, with a covered pot of the dumplings they knew Maya adored.

"So Livvie got her cast taken off, and Elena broke up with me."

"Yay, Livvie Bug! And I don't think she broke up with you. This is your first fight, May."

Maya rubbed her fingers over her eyes, leaving her palms against her face to hide her mortification.

"I said the L word and she told me to get out."

"Lesbians?"

"Winling..."

"Sorry. Tell me again what she said when you told her you were sorry, and it came from the right place even if you were wrong and stuff?"

Maya scrubbed at her puffy eyes and moved to pick at another dumpling. She was already full to bursting and vaguely aware she was eating her feelings.

"Something about how if I pitied her then there was no future for us."

She stuffed some more of the dough into her mouth, defiant, ignoring Winling's brown eyes on her as she did so.

"So basically, you tried to be considerate. In hindsight, knowing how independent Elena is, it may not have been the best plan, but as a result a bunch of old white guys patronized her and treated her like crap, but you're the one she can't forgive?"

Maya nodded glumly.

"She probably made the old guys pee their pants before she left too though. Apparently, they sat her beside the disabled bathroom."

Winling winced.

She picked at the hem of the baggy T-shirt she had thrown on after she arrived home, intending to spend her pity party comfortably.

"I should have seen this coming, I mean, a woman like Elena with someone like me. I was so stupid. Sooner or later it was going to end."

The bowl of dumplings was removed from the table, and she looked after them longingly. Winling spoke as they wrapped it up and put it away, and Maya knew they were probably about to say something she wouldn't want to hear. Her friend had a habit of moving around while delivering bad news.

"With an attitude like that, it definitely won't last. You have to start believing you're good enough for Elena. She believes it so you should too. I mean look at me and Alicia."

Maya could see her point. Alicia was the daughter of the wealthy restaurant owner who Winling worked for as their head chef. The girl was a princess in every way: gorgeous, wealthy, a little spoiled, and completely straight right up until a chance encounter with Winling at a family party she was catering, and the rest was history.

"You probably should have checked with her before you disclosed anything about her disability, it wasn't yours to tell, *but* on the flip side I know you and I know you've been worried about her and I see why you said something."

Winling was right and she hung her head.

"But Maya, don't you think Elena is angry at the wrong person here? You gave them the heads up but what they did with it, that was all on them, and it wasn't like they weren't going to notice something was different from what you've told me. It's visible, right?"

Maya nodded.

"I guess so, I just...never really notice it anymore. She's so much more than that and she just does this thing where she walks in and suddenly owns the room and it's so easy to look past it and never notice how hard she tries underneath all that."

Winling gave her a look.

"What?"

"Girl, you've got it bad."

"Yep, and then she dumped me."

"Maya."

"Winling...I practically told her that I love her, and she told me to get out."

They threw up their hands.

"Guess that's it then. If you're sure it's over what else is there to discuss?"

Maya was being childish, and she knew it.

"May, you know she's sensitive about this, and I remember after the first time you met her and thought she was terrifying, and *super fucking hot though you definitely didn't have a crush on her*—your words by the way. She was wrong to take this out on you, but you know she's embarrassed, pride dented, probably hurt pretty bad by the whole thing. But you're just as bad."

She had been nodding along, agreeing wholeheartedly with everything her friend was saying until that last part.

"Me?"

"Yes. If this was anyone else, Maya, you would have called them on their shit. Just because Elena is disabled doesn't mean she gets to act like this to someone who really cares about her. She can be upset with you for talking about it without asking her, but the reaction you're describing goes way beyond that, and if it was anyone else you would have told them so and talked some sense into them and from the stories you've told me about her, ended up having kinky office sex, *again*."

They did have a point.

"She's obviously embarrassed and angry and pushing you away, but you're just as bad. Rather than standing up and straightening it out, you let her. You got scared and ran again."

They were quiet for a while, and Maya let the truth of the words seep into her psyche. They were right: in any other situation she would have stood up for herself. She knew she had owed Elena an apology for talking about her CP without making sure that was what she wanted, but she hadn't deserved the full force of her anger which she was sure was actually created by the way the men at the company had acted. Elena didn't want to be treated differently, and Maya honestly hadn't thought she had ever done that, but in this instance, she had. She had backed down because the fight was about her disability.

"I'm getting dressed. I have to go."

Winling kicked up their feet and flicked on the TV, apparently staying.

"Call me tomorrow and tell me how it works out?"

*

Her conviction had cooled on the car ride to Elena's house, but she forced herself to be brave. She climbed the steps two at a time, giving herself no time to stop or think before knocking loudly on the door. She told herself not to wring her hands as she waited for an answer.

"Maya?"

Elena was still in her work clothes, a tailored silk blouse and a tight pencil skirt that Maya had drooled over many times hugging her curves.

"Can I come in?" She pushed on, keeping her cool, determined to stay in control of her emotions this time and say what she wanted to say. Elena was so familiar—the smell of her shampoo as she stepped past her into the hall, the tap of her heels as she moved to close the door—and all of it overwhelmed her.

They stood there in awkward silence, Elena avoiding her gaze, her shoulders jerking erratically causing her feet to wander and leaving her not quite standing on the same spot.

"I came to tell you that you're right." Finally, Maya found her voice and for better or for worse, she let the words pour out. She loved all of Elena, and she couldn't be so afraid of saying the wrong thing or doing the wrong thing regarding her CP anymore, because that was a part of her too.

"I did treat you differently, but not when I made that phone call. Tonight, when I let you yell at me, and throw all the blame for what those men did on me, I gave you a pass."

Elena was studying her, dark eyes unreadable, and she pressed on.

"I had no right to tell anyone anything about your CP and I'm sorry. The intention behind it doesn't make what I did right, but I do hope you believe that it came from a good place. I hope you can forgive me for that."

She slicked her now clammy palms over the smooth denim of her jeans, ignoring the tremble in her voice.

"I am so sorry for the way they treated you." She forced herself to be brave as she struggled to continue, the hole burning around the edges as Elena stood in front of her, heartbreakingly beautiful, her eyes shining, making Maya realize so poignantly that she could really have lost her. "But you don't get to yell at me and be mad with me for what *they* chose to do with the information."

She deflated. Finally having said what she came to say, she waited, and she had never felt smaller.

Elena swallowed hard, the sound clearly audible in the silence of the large hallway.

"You're right. I'm so sorry, Maya. For all of this."

She ran her fingers through her hair and Maya had to physically resist the urge to go to her.

"There's no excuse for my behavior. All I can say is that this is something I have struggled with, something that has caused problems in all my relationships to date."

Maya's heart fell.

"I was raised by two people who didn't believe in can't. They told me I could do anything, and then they made me work until that was true. They gave me every opportunity to better myself and never treated me any differently from my sister, never treated me like I was disabled."

She struggled over the word, her face twisting like it tasted bitter in her mouth.

"I don't really think of myself that way, and you were right earlier. I do have to fight for everything, and I think I'm just so used to fighting that when someone else steps in to help me, I don't know how to respond."

She paused, running her tongue over still-red lips before she sucked in another breath.

"I was wrong to take my anger out on you, and I'm sorry for that. I care for you deeply but today made me realize that trying to keep you would just be unfair to us both."

"What?"

Maya's blood turned to ice. This was not supposed to be happening. Somehow, they had resolved the issue, but she was still losing her? Tears pricked the back of her eyes. The urge to cry crashed over her and she tried to swallow it back down.

"I'm significantly older than you Maya, I'm... disabled."

She could hear the tears Elena was fighting as they threatened to spill, her own dangerously close.

"You're young, beautiful, you have everything going for you. You can do so much better than me, sweetheart."

"Are you fucking kidding me?" Maya exploded. She crossed the space between them in two quick strides and took Elena's face in her hands, steadying her until she could look in her eyes. "Fuck you, Elena Mars. Just...fuck you. You don't get to decide what I deserve. You don't get to decide what I am or am not worthy of, because I'm absolutely capable of doing that for myself."

The words were resonating with something deep inside her own psyche, and with the situation reversed, she was suddenly doing her best to convince herself, not just Elena, that she was, in fact, worthy of their relationship.

"I'm going to make more mistakes, but I am trying, and I will try because I...love you. If you don't want me then say so, but don't use the excuse that I deserve better because it's a poor one. Do you want to be with me?"

Elena was crying, tears trailing down her cheeks and soaking Maya's hands as she held her there.

She nodded and Maya pulled her into a tight hug.

"Of course, I want you."

Elena's words were barely above a whisper, and she trembled harder than usual. Maya held on tighter, keeping them in balance.

"I'm sorry I'm such a bitch."

They parted slightly and Maya kissed her hard and then softer.

"Don't push me away?" The question was quiet. Elena nodded her compliance, and Maya could almost physically feel another barrier between them fall away.

Chapter Eleven

There was no other word to describe how Elena had been since that night other than doting. Soft kisses on the back of her neck hidden in the copy room, shared car rides to and from work, and the night she had slept over, the way she had made love to Maya was the most tender she had ever been. There was almost something dark in being intimate with Elena, something claiming in her kisses, something rich and consuming in the way she handled her body and that had still been there, even in the background of the sweetest of moments, making Maya realize it was one of the many things that had her so addicted.

Their night had been a long one. Elena had asked her to attend an only marginally important benefit with her. The event had been a fancy dinner with many people Maya, and apparently Elena, too, didn't know, though most of them seemed to know her. Dressed in an outfit Elena had loaned her, she had never felt more out of place, an imposter walking among people with far more money than she would ever have to her name. Elena apparently sensed her mood, making a five-thousand-dollar donation to the charity—Maya had reread the little numbers on the check three times—and leading her out to the car that waited for them before the event was really over.

The screen designed to block the driver from view was up, and alone with her girlfriend for the first time that night, Maya could finally breathe.

"Not your thing?"

Elena's voice was gentle as she reached up a shaking hand to scratch Maya's scalp though the jerking meant she was sort of tugging on her locks with the action, and Maya found she liked it.

"It was okay. I was just looking forward to ending the night with you, alone."

She smiled up at Elena through her lashes, waiting for those dark eyes to turn black, for the fingers in her hair to tighten, wanting the dark and the dirty and the illicit that came with Elena's need to have her exactly as she pleased.

A soft kiss brushed the corner of her mouth and she sighed.

Things had mended since their fight; they had been fine, wonderful even, but Elena was walking on eggshells. She was being careful, tempering herself in a way that Maya realized she absolutely loathed.

"You're not going to break me, you know?" She whispered the words, the ghost of that sweet kiss still on her lips, making her feel even more perverted for what she truly wanted.

"What do you mean?" A sliver of *her Elena* stirred in the depths of those words and it sent a spike of arousal right into the pit of her belly.

"You've been so sweet to me." She reached up to tangle her fingers in the fine hair at the base of Elena's neck. "It's been amazing, but sometimes..."

Shyness crippled her, but she forced herself onwards.

"Sometimes it's not what I want."

Elena's tremor had their thighs bumping softly, Elena watching her mouth as it formed the words before she raised her gaze back to Maya's eyes. The predator staring back at her made Maya's heart pound with joy.

"Well, what do you want, sweetheart?"

"I want you to fuck me."

She was getting better at dirty talk, though her cheeks still colored spectacularly whenever she attempted it.

"My beautiful girl"—Elena kissed one hot cheek and then the other—"we've fucked almost every day this week."

It was true, but Maya knew she had held back. She also knew Elena knew exactly what she wanted, exactly what she had meant, and the fact she was engaging, playing the game, told her she was closer to getting it than she had come in days. Elena slid a shaking hand up over the smooth black material of her dress and palmed her breast roughly through it.

"What exactly do you want, Maya?"

Liquid heat was spilling back into her veins. Elena was good in bed, good on her desk, good against the wall and on the floor. She was good no matter how they did it, but she had been keeping this part of herself contained, the dark part, the controlling part, and seeing it now, hearing it slick in her voice, Maya's body was alive in a way it just hadn't been during their previous encounters.

She hummed a soft moan as cruel fingers pinched her nipple, tugging on it with the jolt of Elena's arm, her head falling back, lips parted.

"Pull your skirt up." Elena whispered the words, hot into her mouth. Their noses bumped as Maya promptly lifted her hips and did as she was told, cold air hitting her hot flesh through her panties almost painfully.

Elena pulled back to spend a sinfully long few seconds studying Maya's exposed, open legs, eyes lingering on the black satin that covered her, her dress hiked up obscenely around her waist. Apparently pleased, she leaned back in, nipping her ear as she dropped words into it.

"Do you want me to take you right here in the car?"

"Yes."

"With the driver just on the other side of that screen while I fuck you like the filthy girl you are?"

"Yes."

She was mortified, but more so, she was aroused, her thighs slick, her nipples straining against the lace of her bra, because this was her Elena, and she had missed her all week, terribly.

Her panties were pulled aside roughly on the second try and she yelped.

"Say it, Maya."

A flush colored her chest, springing up her neck and onto her cheeks.

"Fuck me like the filthy girl I am, please."

One finger pushed into her, the intrusion pleasurable, and Elena kissed her long and hard, biting her lip as she curled the digit inside. Maya was already panting.

"Like this, sweetheart?"

Those big brown eyes were wide and faux-innocent as they watched her, the tip of her finger tapping her somewhere inside that made her clench hard. She had no idea if the slight movement was intentional or because of Elena's tremor, but it wasn't enough.

"M-more..."

She stuttered out the word.

"More?" That rich, raspy voice repeated her word, softly mocking. "My sweet, greedy girl. There's one condition."

Her hips were rocking against Elena's hand, her orgasm building nicely already, and she nodded her agreement, not caring what it was.

"Don't you dare come."

Shit.

Elena's mouth covered hers, all teeth and tongue and all-consuming, that single finger inside her not enough, pumping, slipping out accidentally as Elena jerked, sending Maya's hips flying off the seat chasing it, before she pushed her down again, a vicious smile on her mouth.

Her hips moved in a frantic rhythm, and she wondered about how serious Elena had been earlier. She was fucking her hard, long deep strokes broken by short shallow ones that made her jaw clench, a soft wet sound accompanying each thrust, a breathy groan in her ear as Elena rubbed herself through her dress, and then her walls were fluttering and she was balancing on the edge.

Elena jerked away as if she was burned and Maya actually whimpered at the loss of her, the loss of the earth-shattering orgasm she had been waiting for all week. The finger was pulled from inside her, and she was suddenly exposed, laid back on a damp leather seat, legs spread, underwear still yanked aside, her orgasm dying a hard death between her shaking legs.

Elena shook in the seat beside her, her body as still as it could be as she watched Maya.

"You broke my rule."

The darkness in her voice as she said the words almost made Maya come on the spot.

She reached shamelessly between pale legs, moving to pull the soaking panties back over Maya's sensitive flesh. It took her two tries to grab the thin material with her shaking fingers, and when she succeeded, she forced her legs together and patted her hip until Maya's bottom was lifted and she could pull her dress down.

"We'll deal with that when we get home."

And God, she was silent for the rest of the car ride leaving Maya stewing in the most frustrating and delicious way, anticipation and a dash of nerves mixing to create a surprising aphrodisiac.

When the car pulled to the curb, Elena thanked the driver and Maya was led without preamble through the dark house, back to Elena's room.

A lamp clicked to life, and Elena stepped into her space and kissed her, softer but with an abandon that told Maya they were not through.

"If you want to stop, you only ever have to say so."

Holy shit this was happening, and she wasn't even entirely sure what *this* was.

"Toys?"

Maya swallowed hard and nodded.

"I um. It's been a while, I've never..."

She fumbled over how to tell Elena she'd not had more than two fingers inside her since Livvie was born.

"We don't have to." Her voice was soft, and Maya knew she was in control, something about having this dialogue open putting her at ease.

"I want to. Just...gentle?"

Elena was looking down at her like she was the most desirable thing in the world, and it made her head spin.

"Of course." She sealed the promise with another soft kiss.

"Spanking?"

Fuck.

"No idea?"

She really had to find the balls to talk to Elena about all this at some point. She had always seemed more dominant between the sheets. Was Elena some secret dominatrix? Maya doubted it but she did feel totally out of her depth and sexually inexperienced faced with these choices.

Elena nodded and Maya watched as she struggled out of her dress, teetering precariously as she wrangled the garment over her head before kicking off her heels and regaining her balance and then shooting her a panty-melting look.

"On the bed, Miss Scott."

God, her voice was all business, and Maya was sure she was going to both love and loathe the flashbacks she was sure to have of this moment every time she heard it at the office from now on.

Clad in just her matching gray lace underwear, Elena disappeared into her closet, leaving her to perch on the edge of the bed, kick off her heels, and wonder if she should take off her clothes too.

When she returned she shoved some items under one of the plush pillows, obscuring them from Maya's view, before she made her way to the head of the bed and lay down, summoning her to join her with one long finger.

"Are you nervous, sweetheart?"

Fingers twisted in her curls, gently tugging her head up so she was looking into Elena's eyes. She moved to nod but realized she couldn't.

"A little."

"Is this what you wanted?"

She swallowed hard.

"I want you to let loose. Don't hold back with me, baby."

She pushed forward to kiss Elena, and she was allowed the movement. Their tongues pressed hot against each other, and then fingers in her hair guided her head back to the pillow.

"Take off your panties."

She did, tossing them to the floor and letting her legs fall apart when Elena tugged up her dress and pushed on the inside of her thigh.

A finger slipped back into her without warning, a strangled sound of surprise becoming a moan. She closed her eyes embarrassed as Elena smiled down at her.

"Where were we?"

It took Maya a second to realize she was supposed to answer, lost again in the feeling of Elena inside her.

"I was um...coming."

Soft lips brushed her cheek and then Elena was disappearing, moving down the bed with some difficulty. Before Maya could really comprehend what was happening, teeth nipped her hip bone, surprising her, sending her lower half shooting off the mattress. Elena's hot mouth on her sex pushed her back down and she keened long and loud at the feeling.

She twisted her fingers in Elena's hair and she lost track of time. The jerking of Elena's body made the act messy, loud slurping and teeth bumping, and Maya loved it. The single finger inside her became two and she moaned her approval. Again and again, Elena brought her close to the edge, tantalizingly so, and just as she was ready to fall, the stimulation died, slowing down, until she was backing away.

She cried out, frustrated, and Elena's mouth left her altogether, appearing above her and covering her own, forcing her tongue between her teeth and letting her taste herself in the kiss.

"I think you're ready."

Maya's head was still spinning as Elena took her hand and wrapped it around something firm and rubbery.

"Will that be okay?"

Forcing herself to focus, she looked down at the toy in her hand, slim and not overly large, and her blood pressure spiked as she realized Elena was going to use it on her. She uttered a shy yes, looking over at Elena who was reclined, her own panties removed, fingers shamelessly rubbing herself.

"Take off my bra and your clothes."

Maya did as she was asked, trying not to stare at the jerking hand between smooth thighs as she fiddled with the front clasp of Elena's bra, and undressed faster than she ever had in her life.

"My sweet Maya."

Elena's eyes were hooded, her tone lazy and full, and Maya wished she had even an ounce of Elena's body confidence as she so obviously waited to make sure Maya's eyes were on her, before she slid the bulb of the toy inside herself. She sunk her white teeth into a kiss-swollen lip, and Maya couldn't help but lean forward and taste the moan that came from her mouth, one hand wrapping around the other side of the toy, using it to move the piece inside her and elicit more of those sounds.

She shifted to hover over Elena, pressing her breasts into Elena's larger ones, kissing her neck, licking a hot trail up to her ear on pure instinct, pleased when she was rewarded with a bruising grip on her ass.

"Oh Maya."

Elena breathed her name, and she kissed her cheek softly in response.

"What is it, baby?"

She could see why Elena loved this, the little thrill of the power that came with laying her open, making her want it, making her feel good.

Elena's hand gripped her thigh, pulling her leg up and over so that she was straddling Elena fully, cool fingers dipping between her legs and stroking her up and down, still drenched from earlier, before she was being guided downwards.

Nerves fluttered in her chest as she reluctantly let the toy go, already missing working on Elena, and lowered her hips as prompted. She had expected Elena to push it inside her. Instead, she was guided down until she was sitting on top of it, the length of it flat against Elena's body between her legs. When gentle hands moved to her hips and pushed her back and then pulled her forward, running her up and down it, Maya felt a new wave of wetness spilling from her.

Elena's body jerked under her, and she wasn't sure how much of that was from the pleasure of the toy moving inside her as she rubbed against it, or her CP. Their mouths moved easily, and Elena kept one hand on her hip, directing her movements, pleasuring them both.

A soft whistle and a loud smack sent pain blooming across her right ass cheek. Maya jumped in surprise, her eyes stinging automatically at the pain, though as an insistent hand pushed her back along the length of the toy it quickly turned to something pleasurable.

"Are you okay, darling?"

Elena was breathless as she looked up at her, and Maya nodded, too shy to tell her exactly how good it felt. Anticipation was pushing her fast toward the edge and she was suddenly busy wondering where the hand that had just struck her was.

Instead of prompting her from her hip, Elena's fingers tangled in her hair, and tugged ever so slightly, and then tugged some more probably accidentally.

"Do you think you deserve to be spanked again?"

She nodded, bracing herself for the blow, rubbing faster up and down the silicone between them, seeing the effects on Elena's face as she bit her lip.

"Use your words."

"Yes, I deserve to be spanked."

She braced again but a blow never landed, and all this anticipation had her heart beating like crazy.

"Why?"

As she was formulating the words, a palm came down again in the same spot hard, catching her just as she pushed back against the toy, a sharp sound of pleasurable pain leaving her as the sting faded.

"Because I was a bad girl."

She didn't even have the presence of mind left to be embarrassed.

A soft tug in her hair jerked her head up and Elena looked her dead in the eyes.

She spanked her again and Maya keened, conscious of Elena holding her steady and watching her react. A long moment passed and she moved frantically against the toy, and then Elena spanked her again and again, tears in her eyes spilling down her cheeks even as she could hear her own voice begging Elena not to stop, her orgasm crashing so close within reach.

One more blow landed across her ass, and just as her body clenched, ready to come, she was forced up, losing contact with the toy, whining pitifully, turning accusing eyes up to a smirking Elena. They stayed like that for a long moment, Maya shifting to balance her own weight on her knees, Elena's jerking the only movement in the room.

"I love you, sweetheart."

It caught her off guard, and Maya was worried she was going to cry again, her chest full to bursting, riddled with endorphins and overcome by the evening. She smiled down at her, not trusting her voice.

Elena smiled back for a long moment, tender, as she reached between them and struggled to move the toy. Understanding what was happening, Maya lifted her own hips.

"Take your time."

She leaned down to kiss this crazy, intense woman who overwhelmed her in so many ways, grateful for the jerky fingers brushing over her clit as she lowered herself slowly down, making them both them moan.

She rode her way to a toe-curling orgasm and then reached down between them and rubbed Elena hard as she continued to move, Elena coming apart, and Maya following with her again until she collapsed on top of her, spent.

Cool fingers brushed sweat-damp hair off the back of her neck as their breaths began to even out.

"Want to take a shower, baby?"

Maya's voice was quiet, reverent, contentment shimmering softly around them in the face of what had just happened.

Elena snickered softly and her words slurred slightly as she spoke.

"That may have to wait until morning. I'm honestly not sure I can stand."

Chapter Twelve

The month of the staff party rolled around fast, and Maya could hardly believe she had already completed almost nine months at TMF. She wiped her sweating palms on her jeans again and forced herself to take another sip of her cooling coffee.

"So sorry I'm late!"

She was surprised when a tall woman with bright-red streaks in her hair slipped into the booth in front of her.

"Um, it's no problem. Thank you for coming."

The woman stuck out her hand.

"I'm Ruby. You must be Maya."

She nodded, trying not to let her discomfort show on her face.

It turned out Ruby was an extremely good family lawyer, not just because Elena had told her so, but also because it was obvious from the way she spoke about the system. Maya was pleasantly surprised to find that she liked Ruby and thrilled she would be working with her in the custody battle.

"It looks to me like you're in great stead, Maya. You have a well-paying job which you've held down for almost a year—it should be a year by the time our date comes up— you have a car and a steady place to live in a decent part of town. You've thought about schools and Livvie already has a savings account with some money earmarked for college. She sounds like a lucky little girl."

Maya returned Ruby's encouraging smile with a shy one, which she had to quickly catch before it become a grimace as she remembered the next question she had to ask.

"Thank you so much, Ruby. Do you charge hourly or...?"

She reached for the checkbook she had shoved in her pocket from her overnight bag as she'd left Elena's that morning, bracing herself for the cost. The guy she had hired to represent her the first time around had made her weekly salary in about three hours, and she had still lost.

"Oh, no worries, babe! You're with Elena so you're practically family. Just make me the cool aunt once we get all this taken care of?"

Maya was flabbergasted.

"Of course, but I really can't let you just... I have no—"

Elena's fingers settled over hers and her kind eyes searched out Maya's until she would hold them.

"Maya, you got stiffed. Elena didn't tell me the whole story, she said it wasn't hers to tell, but I know Robert Holt and I know he doesn't always play fair. Let me help you?"

Taking a deep breath, she tried to exhale the guilt she felt over accepting the insanely generous offer.

"Okay, but once this is over, I'm taking you out to dinner."

Ruby hooted a laugh. "I'm bringing my wife, you bring Elena, and we'll make a night of it!"

*

She arrived back at what she had taken to referring to affectionately in her head as "the mansion" and pushed open Elena's big old front door that had become familiar over the previous months. The sound of voices wound down the hall to greet her, and she followed them back to the kitchen, enjoying the few moments she could catch of her girlfriend and her daughter together, both entirely oblivious to her presence.

"But why?"

It was Livvie's favorite question lately, and if Maya was being honest, she loved having someone to share fielding the answers with.

"Well, the recipe only called for the yolks, do you remember what we read in the book?"

Elena's back was to her, and judging from the strings tied around her waist, she was wearing an honest to God apron, and baking with her kid. Maya didn't think she could ever love anyone more.

The kitchen looked like a war zone. Flour covered the usually pristine granite countertops, and she noticed a puddle of batter on the floor, guessing either Elena or Livvie had knocked the first batch on the ground and they were having to start over.

"Look, what's the first letter?"

They were hunched over a book Maya couldn't see, Livvie's hair in a long slightly messy braid, her flour-covered hand fisted in the side of Elena's blouse keeping her balanced on the bucket she was standing on.

"E?"

"Yes, very good, and what about this one?"

They were quiet for a long time and Maya marveled again at how natural Elena was at all this, how easy it seemed for her. She thought of things that didn't occur to Maya; she was always focused on having fun and just enjoying the precious time she got with her daughter, but Elena was always thinking, always teaching her, and nurturing her. It made Maya wish she could be better.

"It's a *G*, *G* for game!"

"I don't know that one, Mm'lena."

"That's all right, you knew the *E*."

"Like my *E* for Livvie."

She could watch them like this all day. As much as Elena made her feel insecure about her own parenting skills, Maya forced herself not to think that way. If anything, she should be glad Livvie had another amazing adult in her life who wanted to spend time with her and do these kinds of things with her.

"So you see, the book says egg, E-G-G, and the next word is yolks, so we only need to use the yolks, the yellow parts."

She heard Elena's sigh of relief when the reasoning was deemed good enough, and she wondered exactly how many more "whys" her girlfriend had been faced with since she'd left that morning.

They continued adding ingredients to the bowl, and Elena was struggling to beat them together, shaky hands sending batter spilling over the sides, when finally, she was spotted.

"Mama!"

Livvie's shrill greeting told her she had been missed, though the brownies were still more exciting, apparently, and she stayed by Elena's side watching her move the whisk around the bowl.

"Miss Scott, did no one ever tell you it's rude to eavesdrop?"

Her dark eyes glittered with a happiness Maya just loved to see there.

"Rude to vevesop, Mama," Livvie parroted back, and Elena snickered into the bowl.

"What are you guys making?" She ignored the fact that her daughter seemed so heavily influenced by Elena, unsure if it was the best or worst thing ever, and moved to take the bowl from Elena's shaking hands. She scraped the powder that still clung to the edges into the mixture and set about beating it.

Elena stayed quiet, letting Livvie answer. Maya felt a pinch on her hip and looked up into her soft brown eyes, wishing she could lean up and kiss her. She wanted to talk to Livvie about their relationship soon; she just hadn't found the right moment yet.

"Well, Liv, what are we making?"

She asked the question again, getting Livvie's attention from the shapes she'd been drawing in the flour spilled on the counter.

"Brownies."

"Aww, you guys didn't have to make all these brownies for me! That's so nice! I can't wait to eat every... single...one."

Elena shoved her playfully and Livvie looked devastated at the development.

"No, Mama, not all for you, just somes for you, 'kay? Somes for Mama but then somes for me and My'lena."

The development of that nickname didn't surprise Maya, but she heard Elena's breath catch audibly in her throat.

"For you and who else?" She hoped to get Livvie to repeat it, and she was rewarded with a swooping hand gesture toward the woman in question like it was the most obvious answer in the world.

"My'lena. Her wants some, and I want some."

"Okay, kid. I'll share the brownies."

Elena seemed to have recovered.

"Yes, you will, Miss Scott," she offered darkly before she turned to Livvie. "It's *she* wants some, darling, not *her* wants some. Do you understand?"

Livvie nodded, looking up at Elena with wide green eyes, a sweet moment passing between them. Elena smiled down at her with a fondness that melted Maya's heart, and then Livvie spoke again.

"But why?"

*

It still felt surreal, lying in Elena's huge bed beside her, Livvie tucked in the guest room, for now.

"What are you thinking about, sweetheart?" Elena's voice was soft and warm and as welcoming as the entire day had been. She didn't dare to let herself hope, but despite that, she knew she was—she could so easily get used to this.

"Just how great today was." She chose to keep the rest to herself, not wanting to taint the last of a wonderful evening with her insecurities.

Elena hummed in response.

"How was your meeting with Ruby?"

"Great. She was not what I expected at all, she was actually so much better."

Elena laughed.

"Is your date set?"

Nerves fluttered in Maya's stomach.

"Yes, December 3."

"Just in time for Christmas."

A content silence hung between them, easy in a way Maya found it to be with so few people.

"Today was wonderful, with Livvie, and with you."

"It was," Maya agreed.

"My life is full in a way I never thought it would be."

Feeling Elena move to roll onto her side, Maya quickly pushed up onto her elbow, turning and leaning there so they were face to face, sparing Elena the trouble of wrangling her tired body into cooperating. She let her pale fingers trace a path down Elena's smooth cheek and waited for her to go on, seeing the unspoken words in her eyes.

"I never thought... It's wonderful to feel like a part of your family, just for a little while."

It still made no sense to her how Elena could see herself as a burden, as someone incapable of belonging in a family unit, despite the fact she was the most nurturing person Maya had ever met.

"Not just for a little while, for always...if you want?" She stumbled over the last part as she realized the breadth of the offer she was making, suddenly worried that Elena would think it too much, though she couldn't deny that behind her own fear, she wanted it, badly.

Elena's eyes were already shining by the time she answered, and for once, she didn't hide her weakness.

"I'd like that very much."

Maya's heart soared, and she leaned down to kiss her gently, their noses bumping with Elena's tremor as she hovered so their lips were a hairsbreadth apart, before stealing one more kiss.

"I've been meaning to talk to Livvie about it and explain about us. Maybe we can do it together next time we have her?"

She could see the happiness burst behind Elena's eyes at her inclusion in having Livvie from now on.

"If you're sure, darling, I don't want you to feel rushed, and I want to do what's best for Livvie. I'm fine with just being the family friend who likes tea parties and shakes all the time."

Maya laughed softly and then grew serious.

"But you're not, you're so much more than a family friend. I love you, Elena. You're my partner and you're a part of this family, messed up as it is, if you want to be. I want Livvie to know that. I'm pretty sure she's going to be over the moon once she understands. It just may take her a while."

Elena nodded, a shy smile that Maya so rarely got to see kissing her lips.

"Okay."

*

Looking back, Maya should have known. She was always so careful, always conscious of the way some things were just too good—not too good to be true, but too good to belong to someone like her. That perfect moment, the perfect evening, the entire perfect day with Elena and Livvie, it was never going to last. If she hadn't been so under Elena's spell, so intoxicated by her, high on this new beautiful life that had felt so wonderfully within her reach, she probably would have seen it coming.

"May, do you even want to go to this thing? Maybe you should just sit this one out, we can go out somewhere else or stay in, or whatever, and you can talk to Elena tomorrow and work it out."

She gritted her teeth, steely eyes staring back at her in the mirror as she continued to curl her hair.

"It's my work party, too, my friends will be there, and honestly, why should I be the one who has to miss it because Elena's acting like an ass?"

Winling didn't reply, suddenly busy again talking softly to Alicia, Alicia's pitchy little giggles floating to Maya's ears, frustrating her. It wasn't that she didn't like her best friend's girlfriend; usually they got on well, but tonight she was just too fucking happy, and Maya wanted to punch someone.

"I just can't believe her." She knew she was repeating herself but fuck it, Winling and Alicia were making out on her couch while she fixed her hair in the mirror by the front door, and it wasn't like they were really listening anyway. "Here I am, ready to tell my three-year-old about us, and she, a grown-ass woman, not only refuses to tell her mother but agrees to go to the company party with a *date* her mother picked out for her."

Neither of them replied.

"Oh, it won't mean anything, Maya. It's just a meaningless party, Maya." She did a poor imitation of Elena and immediately felt bad about it. Steeling herself, she pressed on. "Am I wrong to be upset that the woman I've been dating, almost living with, who I introduced my daughter to and started a freaking life with, against all of my better judgment, is too ashamed of me to take me to the office party and would rather go with some rich perfect woman her mother chose for her?"

The two finally parted, and Alicia seemed to take pity on her.

"I know if they did that, they would find themselves without a girlfriend."

She pushed Winling's shoulder gently, causing them to raise their hands in defense and add, "But it is a different situation. We know Elena's life is pretty different than ours, and her family are probably really strict or something."

Maya turned furious eyes on Winling and saw her best friend regretting the words. It made her feel good, and it made her feel guilty, but she took the first one and ran with it, feeling horribly entitled to her shitty attitude in the wake of Elena rejecting her invite to go to the party together only to go with another woman.

"But does that make it okay to hide me like some dirty little secret? I don't know if I'm not rich enough or just not pretty enough, not stuck up enough, all I know is I'm *not enough*. I don't belong in her world and I never will. I don't know how I didn't see it before."

Her own words dissolved all her annoyance, tears pricking her eyes, and she was cycling back through hurt and anger again, as she had been all night.

"May..." Winling started but Alicia cut them off, jumping up and moving to stand by Maya in front of the mirror.

"Maya, you look amazing. I'm going to do your makeup. That dress is killer on you, you are *hot*."

All blue eyes and long auburn hair, Alicia was undeniably gorgeous, and dressed in the very expensive popular girl dress she had borrowed from her, Maya felt a little bit of the confidence that came with looking good spilling into her veins.

"Fuck Elena, you're going to have fun tonight. If she thinks you're not good enough then it's her loss. And if this is some stupid...status issue, which eww—"

Maya forced herself not to laugh. Alicia was such a princess at times, oblivious in a way only someone with way too much money could be.

"Then fuck her for that too! You're wearing four thousand dollars of dress, hon."

"Alicia, I really did not need to know that..." The thought of being responsible for something so expensive really had her considering taking Winling's advice and just staying home.

"Burn it when you're done!" Alicia cried, making Maya jump.

"Tonight is about exactly the opposite of that. No more apologetic Maya, no more wondering if she's good enough Maya. Just go there, rock it, own it, and show her what she's missing. I mean she has a gorgeous *much* younger woman who's smart, and funny, and amazing, and she chooses to go to the party with some old hack her mother chose... One, that's creepy. Two—"

The words were buoying her, lifting her spirits, and Maya let them.

"Winling, open the wine in the kitchen, baby, and bring us both a glass."

Alicia turned back to her, two apparently forgotten, as she spun Maya around and pushed her back against the table so she could start on her makeup.

"This is her mistake, Maya. Don't let it ruin your night, just go out there and show her exactly what she's missing. Let her watch you having a great time, and by the end of the evening she will be begging at your feet for you to forgive her and take her home."

Maya could feel the light coming back into her eyes. It all made sense. As disappointed and feeling as burned as she was by Elena's decision, Alicia's words sounded like a revelation, and she clung to them, suddenly determined.

She would show Elena exactly what she was missing.

*

The buzz from the three glasses of wine she'd had with Alicia was still running pleasantly through her veins when she arrived at the party. Elena had rented out an entire club for the event, and Maya was surprised to find more people there than she had anticipated, many of whom she didn't recognize.

The lights were still up, and everyone seemed to be humming around pleasantly, talking, drinking, and warming up for the night. A cursory glance through the bodies did not reveal Elena, and unsure if she was grateful or disappointed she headed for the bar, where she ordered herself a large Jack and Coke and a tequila, because it was an open bar and Elena was paying.

"Maya?"

She turned to see Margaret had appeared behind her.

"Wow, you look absolutely beautiful! My goodness."

Of course, Margaret was wearing a sweet floral number, her short hair combed stylishly to one side, Dave trailing behind her, and not for the first time Maya wondered about their relationship.

"Hey, Margaret, Dave. Who are all these people?"

The two huddled around her, leaning against the bar, voices raised to be heard over the music and the chatter steadily growing in the large space.

"They work on other floors, for some of Cara's other companies. Elena's mother," Margaret offered by way of explanation. The memory of Cara Mars left an unpleasant taste in Maya's mouth; she washed it down with a long swallow of her drink.

"Where is Elena? I wasn't sure if perhaps the two of you might be coming together?"

The question was careful, nonjudgmental. Any other day Maya might have panicked—maybe she would have been glad to finally have the proverbial cat out of the bag—but tonight, she just shrugged.

"Nope." The p popped on her lips. "No idea where she is."

Neither of them pressed the issue any further. They talked and laughed, and Maya ordered two more drinks, Kevin, Kathryn, and Adam joining them. Her evening was progressing nicely, surrounded by work friends, feeling a million dollars in Alicia's expensive dress, shoes, and jewelry. Finally, the heavy feeling in her stomach that had followed her all day began to dissipate, and then the noise level in the room dropped.

She followed the turned heads in the direction of the doors, and the warm glow that had been surrounding her, with Elena momentarily forgotten, fell away, shattering like ice over her head.

In the doorway stood Cara Mars, a man beside her obviously Latin in heritage, who Maya assumed to be Elena's father; and then there was Elena herself. She was stunningly beautiful in that earth-shattering, completely conquering way Maya was totally in love with. Her dark eyes were rimmed in smoky shadow, her jewelry demure but edgy, a sleek burgundy dress hugging her figure perfectly, as she wobbled slightly on ridiculous heels. Mad as she was, Maya's heart still beat hard in her chest at the sight of her, the action turning hot and painful when she noticed the blonde woman beside Elena, one hand disappearing behind her to rest on what she assumed was the small of Elena's back.

Her breath burned hot, the fire inside needing an escape, and it poured out of her, almost choking her.

The other woman was attractive, as much as she loathed to admit it, close to six feet of platinum-blonde glamazon, with a stylish bob, and a level of sophistication Maya knew she could never possess. Undeniably, she looked like she belonged by Elena's side, in her fancy cocktail dress that she probably hadn't had to loan from a friend for the occasion.

She was vaguely aware of the clapping erupting around her, everyone celebrating the family who was throwing the party and signing their paychecks every week, but she couldn't bring herself to join in. Her breathing was loud in her ears and she was as furious as she was broken, crushed by the sight in front of her.

The horrible blonde woman leaned down to whisper something in Elena's ear, smiling at her like she belonged exactly there, beside her, touching her, soaking up the gratitude directed toward her like she was a part of the Mars family already.

She was made for the limelight, for the high life. Cara Mars thought her worthy, and obviously Elena did too. Maya knew she would never be comfortable in that position; she would always be too shy, too insecure, too fucking humble. She would never be right for Elena. The realization crashed over her, knocking the wind out of her. She felt Kevin's breath on the side of her neck as he leaned forward to ask her if she was okay, the clapping subsiding while Cara Mars was saying something into a mic about all their hard work that year.

She was trying to find her breath, trying to find something solid to ground her, regretting the alcohol heavy in her system, bogging her down. She was trying to reply when a pair of dark eyes found her.

Kevin was too close to her, one hand on her hip, asking again if she was all right, and she let the hand stay because *fuck Elena*, fuck her and her money and all her stupid soft eyes and private smiles that had ever made Maya believe she could belong.

"I'm fine." She turned to give Kevin what she hoped was a reassuring smile. He patted her hip and let her go, and when she looked back, Elena and her family were moving over to a booth, and the room was returning to its previous state, the excitement of their arrival done.

The shock of it, the anger, the resentment, the fucking heartbreak, was still pouring through her. Her hands were shaking by her sides, and when Kathryn appeared beside her, mischief in her dark-blue eyes, and slung an arm over her shoulders, Maya tried to lose herself in it.

"Shots?"

Everyone agreed and Kathryn made a large order. Maya downed one and then two, forcing herself not to look for Elena, Alicia's words ringing in her ears.

Somehow tonight, she was going to have fun.

The night wore on, and Kevin became an unlikely ally, the only person in the group not to ask her if she was all right, or suggest she slowed up some. He simply clinked his glass to hers and knocked them back with her, while they both snickered into their chasers at Margaret's disapproving eyes. It felt juvenile, but it also felt good to shuck responsibility and expectation and for once just cut loose, completely.

Kathryn and her husband Frank had disappeared to the dance floor, Margaret and Dave following, leaving Maya squashed between Adam and Kevin at the bar.

"So, tell us, love, what's really going on between you and the boss bitch? I've had a wager with Adam for three months now, and it's time I got paid."

The mention of Elena made Maya sneer. She was in that wonderful phase of angry drunkenness, and it made it so easy not to hurt.

"Please... Me and Elena?"

The words burned so good and they burned so bad, ringing with a truth she chased away with another large swallow of her drink.

"Ha!" Kevin was rowdy in his victory. "Pay up, Adam, told you she's not a lesbian."

Maya opened her mouth to correct him but decided it didn't matter. Right now, she was enjoying their camaraderie, and she didn't feel like rocking the boat.

"Hi."

A female voice interrupted her, followed by a tap on the shoulder, and Maya turned to see a woman she vaguely recognized from her morning elevator rides.

"Hi?" It was a question, but she was laughing, loving how this was shaping up. The woman before her was all cropped sandy hair, athletic build, and a dapper slacks and shirt combo in place of the cocktail dress most of the women were sporting. Maya recognized attraction on someone's face when she saw it, and this was exactly what she needed.

"I'm Hanna. You probably don't know me."

Maya interrupted her, alcohol making her lips loose.

"We ride the elevator together most days. I'm Maya. It's nice to officially meet you."

They talked, laughed, Kevin and Adam growing quiet as they watched the exchange between the two, and Maya was so smug at that development.

When Hanna tugged on her hand to lead her toward the dance floor, she went willingly. Her drink sloshed messily over the edge of the glass, so she downed it and dumped her glass on a table as they passed by.

She tried not to look for Elena as they walked, but she found her, looking absolutely furious, a storm brewing on her face and an anger in her eyes that made Maya think *good.*

Hanna stopped them at a spot on the edge of the floor, and Maya used their joined hands to drag her backward, spying Kathryn and the others through the crowd and moving to join them.

The lights flashed, the music was picking up as the hour grew later, and it was easy to lose herself in it all. To laugh with Margaret, to let Frank twirl her around, to ignore Hanna's hands on her waist, the heat of her body at her back as she danced, shameless, a little dirty, more confident than she had ever been thanks to the way Elena had introduced her to her own sensuality.

"Maya."

A cool hand was firm around her upper arm, and Maya turned to face the interruption, barely able to hear her over the music. Hanna immediately backed away and she could feel the eyes of her coworkers on them.

Elena was furious. It sent a jolt of adrenaline through her body and set her skin on fire, and in that moment, she was lost in it. She wanted Elena to feel some of the hurt she had carried all day, and she wanted her to drag her into the bathroom and break herself against her.

She didn't reply, turning to move back to the group, but Elena held on, stumbling with the movement, pulled off balance easily. Maya caught her and held on just long enough to keep her on her feet before she pulled away.

"I'm busy, Elena." She stood on her tiptoes to let the words fall into Elena's ear. "And don't you have a *date* to entertain?"

She yanked her arm away and went back to her friends, laughing at their stunned faces, continuing to dance, though everyone around her was still staring at the spot where she guessed Elena was still standing. Elena must have left because, finally, they began to dance with her again.

Everything moved around her, blurred by the lights and the beat. Hanna sidled away not long after Elena left, no doubt sensing the drama and not wanting to be involved. Maya didn't care.

Kathryn bounced around with her, their hands swinging between them, Kathryn probably as drunk as she was, and laughing, singing along with the music. For once, Maya felt her age, and honestly it made her feel immature but also free.

Finally, Frank grabbed Kathryn around the waist, steadying her as she swayed, and motioned for Maya to come as he began to steer them back to the group, following behind Margaret and Dave who had gotten tired and left to sit down a while ago.

Irritated that her buzz had been interrupted, but a little dizzy herself, Maya followed. She tripped on an empty bottle, catching herself just in time, ready to take another step toward the booth where their group was sitting, when her eyes caught on Elena's.

She was watching her, sitting at a table, an untouched Martini in front of her, flanked by Cara on one side, and the blonde on the other, murder in her eyes, though beneath it Maya saw a sadness that cut through some of the liquor's haze.

She had no idea how long they had been staring, no idea if anyone had noticed or if the party was going on without her. In that moment, she was connected to Elena, painfully so. All the anger, the sadness, the hurt, burning bright and open, and she thought that maybe, just maybe she could feel an apology in those guarded brown eyes.

She ached for her, suddenly tired, suddenly awake. She wanted to kiss that scowl off her face and take her home and spend all night taking turns repenting for their sins.

Something crept into her awareness, the blonde leaning close to Elena, too close, one hand reaching out and settling high on a bouncing thigh, causing the limb to still. Those brown eyes were still on her, retribution shining in them, one perfect eyebrow slightly raised in a challenge, and then Maya was seeing red all over again.

"There you are, love. I've been trying to catch you alone all night." She barely heard Kevin, too absolutely fucking livid to process anything but that smug look on Elena's face. How *dare* she play that game when she was the one who had caused all this? She forced herself to look away, Kevin a convenient target for her attention that she suddenly needed to have on anything, anything but Elena.

"I know we didn't get off to the best start, and well... Oh fuck it."

Then he was kissing her.

His mouth was insistent in a way that made her stomach turn sour. Where Elena's lips made her feel owned but cherished, his just made her feel dirty, his stubble rough on her chin, his palms clammy on her cheeks. She was frozen, the liquor slowing her reaction, the second where she should have pushed him away passing, and the one after and the one after that as her alcohol-scrambled brain struggled to catch up, struggled to move through the thick treacle of the woman who deserved Elena like she never would, the hand on her thigh, that smug smirk, and now Kevin kissing her... *Kevin kissing her?*

She shoved his shoulders and he backed away obediently, a hope shining in his eyes that made her stomach roll. *Fuck.*

"Kevin, I'm a lesbian. I've been dating Elena since April."

Shit... Elena.

Not caring about Kevin standing open mouthed in front of her, she turned back to find Elena's seat empty, catching the back of her head and a flash of burgundy as she disappeared out of a door.

Ignoring Kevin calling out to her, she took off after Elena, aware even in her intoxication that she had crossed a line, however unwillingly. She had no idea how long Kevin had been kissing her, but she knew it was too long.

She shoved her way through the bodies between her and her destination, ignoring the annoyed shouts that rose in volume behind her as she spilled drinks and tripped on feet, not caring about anything but catching Elena.

"Elena?"

Elena was still making her way down the long hall, the music quiet through the thick wooden doors separating it from the main room. Elena turned her eyes on her, full of tears, totally at odds with the cruel sneer on her lips, and Maya felt weightless, a single sheet of paper already tattered and torn, ready to be tossed around in Elena's storm.

"Leave me alone!" She screamed the words, her voice louder than Maya had ever heard it, horribly distorted, the words slurring and blending, all her usual carefully placed breaths, intonation, control, gone now.

"Elena, he just kissed me."

She tried to move forward, staggering slightly, acutely aware that she was absolutely too drunk to be having this conversation but unwilling to let Elena go.

"And you let him!" She roared the words, and something in Maya woke up, hot and angry.

"And you let Miss Perfect Rich Glamazon hang off you all night! I get it, Elena, I do. She's everything I will never be—wealthy, confident, probably doesn't have a bunch of baggage and a kid."

If she was mad, Elena was madder.

"Don't you dare. I have never, ever, not once regretted you having Livvie. I love her, and I loved you."

"That's why you were too ashamed to go to this stupid party with me?" Maya yelled the words back because screw her and her past tense.

Elena stalked closer, unsteady on her feet.

"If you had checked your damn phone you would know that I already told my parents about you this morning."

The world crashed around Maya, and she was filled with a sick awareness that something had gone horribly wrong.

"I told them this morning that I loved you, that I didn't care what they thought, that I loved Livvie, too, and we were happy, we were going to be a family."

The last word dissolved into a sob, and tears sprang to Maya's eyes.

"I had to come with Robin because it was arranged for weeks, out of politeness and nothing else. I have been trying to tell you all day how sorry I was, how I hated that you thought you were anything less than perfect for me."

She was crying now, actually crying, and Maya was suddenly, painfully sober.

"Elena." She reached for her, fingertips just grazing her arm, her voice soft and apologetic and broken.

"Don't." The word was ice.

"Have you been seeing him all along?" It was a ridiculous accusation, and they both knew it, but Maya could sense Elena was rising up, repairing herself, bitterness and blackness filling all the holes they had blown in each other, until her face was twisted into a mask that Maya recognized but hated.

"What was I to you? A foray into the land of alternative lifestyles? Your charity case? An easy fucking target with plenty of money?"

Maya didn't realize she had slapped her until Elena staggered back. Though the blow wasn't hard, with Elena's compromised balance it was enough to make her stumble and catch herself on the wall for support, and this was all spiraling out of control.

She laughed, a bitter, fractured sound, and gone was the woman Maya had laid in bed with so many nights, the woman who had made her feel so cherished, so safe, who had felt so very permanent in her life.

"Fuck you, Maya Scott."

Every word was a physical blow, and Maya was the one crying now, everything crashing around her as it came to its end.

"Fuck you." Elena's body jumped with the words, and as she walked away, she staggered before righting herself again on the wall, her tremor seemingly intensified by emotion.

She shoved open the door to a fire exit, the cool air pouring in from outside. Maya watched her leave, broken.

Chapter Thirteen

By Monday morning she was barely holding herself together, riding the elevator toward a job she was no longer sure was hers, everything in her life suddenly uncertain again in a way she loathed, but should have expected.

She had woken on Saturday morning to twin punches in the gut. Retrieving the phone she had discarded sometime Thursday evening after their fight, she found a very apologetic text from Elena admitting she was wrong and telling her she had told her parents about their relationship, as well as several more that followed, each growing increasingly worried about her.

After that she had one from Robert, so simple yet effective in its ability to destroy her completely.

> *Maya. Received court summons today. Very disappointed, had hoped we were past this. Olivia will not be available for visits this month; we have family outings planned those weekends. Best to you and Ruby Layton; see you in court.*

Her body still wanted to tremble at the thought of it. Ruby had warned her something like this might happen but with only a month between the summons and the court date, it had seemed a worthwhile gamble to miss Livvie for two weekends and hopefully win her forever. It had seemed bearable with Elena by her side, but now, with her life totally derailed, she was breaking. She hadn't heard from Ruby since the disaster of the party, and the fact Holt knew who was representing her was terrifying, even more so considering she wasn't sure the offer still stood after everything that had happened. She wasn't even sure she still had a job.

The elevator doors opened, and she stepped off, the office silencing at her arrival. She looked around pitifully for Elena.

Margaret rushed for her. She took her by the elbow and turned her around, tugged her up the stairs and out into the hall.

"Maya."

Her voice was full of pity and Maya already knew. She had been so stupid, and she had lost everything. Elena, her job, her lawyer, and any chance at winning her court date now she was once again unemployed, and this time, it was all her own doing. She was already crying, Margaret's voice far away, lost somewhere between her rapidly building sobs. They were choking the life out of her, and she watched from somewhere far away as they sucked all the air out of her lungs. She didn't even fight. She was sitting on the cold floor, her back to the wall, struggling to breathe when a voice cut through the panic.

"Maya..."

Her tone was cool, business at best, and shaky hands squeezed her upper arms, urging her unsteadily to her feet. She felt pathetic, small and vulnerable, and she hated the traitorous hope that burst in her chest as Elena watched her with unreadable eyes. Margaret was gone. She must have left after bringing her here.

"Maya, you have to breathe."

Elena's presence, her voice, was a balm over the fear, the falling, and so she did, drowning herself in those dark eyes she loved until the white walls stopped spinning.

When her breaths evened out, Elena let her go. The panic prickled at the back of her neck again, but watching Elena draw a breath to speak, she fought it.

"You still have a job. You're reassigned to the fourth floor. It's a comparable position with comparable pay and similar duties, working in procurement for my father's clothing company."

She delivered the words impassively, as if she was reading aloud or ordering a coffee.

"When you're ready, take yourself down to the fourth floor, and Harold will get you started. I truly wish you all the best, Maya."

Her voice broke ever so slightly on the last word, a sliver of emotion, a sliver of everything they were, and had been, and were supposed to be, shining through and it both ruined Maya and saved her.

"Elena, please." Her voice was hoarse, and she was begging, her pride long tossed aside. It didn't matter.

Elena looked back at her, dark eyes that she knew so well full of something she couldn't decipher, her head held high, shoulders squared as she met the end that Maya was so sickeningly unprepared for.

"Take care, Miss Scott."

*

She moved like a robot through her day, taking easily to her new duties, losing herself in them, avoiding the eyes of those around her, unsure if she was novel because she was new, or because of what happened at the party.

She cried in the bathroom at lunch, finally getting up the nerve to text Ruby and simply ask her if she was still willing to represent her, offering again to pay her.

A reply didn't come until three days later, when she had all but lost hope, spilling into a sea of numbness, transitioning from work to home keeping everyone out, even Winling who had called, texted, and come knocking at her door more times than Maya could count. She missed Livvie terribly, petrified she had lost her forever through the foolish belief that, somehow, she could be strong enough, good enough, lucky enough, to take on Robert Holt and win. Elena had made her strong, made her brave, showed her a side of herself that Maya hadn't known existed, and in hindsight she could see it was nothing more than a dream, and in comparison, reality was horrifically dim.

"Jesus, you look terrible."

Ruby plopped down in front of her and Maya jumped, spilling the hot coffee she had been pretending to drink all over her hand, though she hardly noticed. She was sure Ruby had asked to meet just to deliver the blow in person, to tell her how shitty she had been, and then tell her she was without a lawyer as well as the many other things that were now lacking in her life. Maya had gone to the coffee shop, anyway, deciding she needed closure. She needed to know for sure that she was as screwed as she felt.

"Maya." Ruby dabbed her hand with a napkin, prying it from around the paper cup and squeezing it tight.

"I'm furious at you but I'm still going to represent you. One, because I'm not a shitty person, and whether you fucked up or not you love your kid and don't deserve to lose her over this, and two, because Elena is insisting that I don't let it color my judgment of you, whatever that means."

Elena. Her name was a gift and a curse, and faced again with her kindness, Maya asked herself how she had ever been stupid enough to lose her before she reminded herself it was what she did. She broke everything she touched, always.

"Has Robert contacted you?"

She could tell Ruby was trying to be cool, distant, and she knew she deserved it. She nodded, pulling out her phone on autopilot and opening the last message before sliding it across the table.

"He's trying to intimidate you, you know that, right? We talked about this and we knew this might happen." Ruby went on and on about Robert rescinding her visits and sticking to their plan, and the words felt scripted, a courtesy read off for each client in her shitty situation. She heard them, she listened, but somehow, they didn't sink inside her, unable to make it past the numbness that had blanketed her like a fog.

"Oh, for fuck's sake." Ruby exploded, making her jump as she slapped her palms on the table, drawing the attention of those around them, though she didn't seem to care. "You're pitiful... Why the hell did you kiss him?"

The accusation shot through her, a jolt through the smog, giving her the strength to reply, the strength, for just a moment, to care.

"I didn't, he kissed me. I was wasted. By the time I shoved him off it was too late."

Ruby studied her, and Maya wondered what she was looking for.

"I fucked up though. I was childish. I should have checked my phone, or just stayed home, or talked it out with her rather than getting wasted and acting out."

They were quiet for a long time and then Ruby sighed.

"Yeah, you should. I've never seen Elena this... messed up."

That admission stung.

"Look, Maya. I like you. She was never happier than when you two were together. I don't know the ins and outs, but I know she still cares about you, I just don't know if she can forgive you. She stood up to her mom for your relationship, which she has rarely ever done, and then... well, you can imagine how what happened afterward made her look."

Ruby cringed and the little spark of hope Maya felt faded.

"I don't know if she will forgive you, but if you still care about her, you should try."

The words shocked her, slicing through the fog and momentarily reviving her. It hadn't occurred to her that there was anything beyond this. As far as she had thought it was over, done, past, but perhaps Ruby was right.

She wanted to try, as scared to hope as she was, but she had no idea where to start. Elena had completely iced her out. She had blocked her number, exiled her from the office, and made her desire that she leave her alone pretty clear. Too tired to explain it all to Ruby, to continue to cling to impossibilities, she just nodded.

*

Two weeks floated by. Margaret had texted her twice, first asking how the new job was going, and the second time asking if she was all right. Maya wondered what they all thought of her now, her old coworkers, her old friends.

She'd finally given up and let Winling in a week ago after another extended knocking session complete with threats to break down the door, or worse, call Elena.

Maya had cried until she was hoarse, poorly explaining the whole thing and then making Winling promise to never bring it up again. She fell asleep while they were watching *Friends* reruns, her best friend's hand squeezed in hers—a Band-Aid on the wreck of the life that didn't last.

She trudged faster down the dimly lit street, unsure how long she had been walking. She'd been breaking for a while, coming apart quietly, out of her own line of sight. What had finished off her sanity tonight was another phone call, an attempt to call Robert, one he miraculously answered for a change. He was smug in his condolences about her relationship with Elena, self-assured and overconfident as he told her *Olivia* was unavailable and would be until after the court date and likely indefinitely, so to please stop calling. It was almost enough to wake her up, to make her angry, to tempt her to get up and push back, but what was there to do?

So, she walked, pounding out her frustrations on the sidewalk, thankful to be anywhere but alone, suffocating in her apartment that was too empty without Livvie, without Elena.

"Excuse me, do you have the time?"

She hadn't noticed someone walking up behind her, passing her on the sidewalk before they turned, walking backward as they asked the question. The guy was about her age, maybe a little older, a ball cap half obscuring his face.

"Uh, sure…" Her voice was scratchy from underuse and she cleared her throat, pulled her phone from her pocket, and read off the illuminated screen.

"Eleven twenty-five."

"Thanks." He carried on walking, and Maya nodded, shoving the phone back into her pocket.

Suddenly all the air left her chest, her back colliding hard with a wall as she was pushed into the mouth of an alley. Panic gripped her, cutting through the fog and leaving her hyperalert after weeks of numbness. She was painfully aware of how much weight she had lost, how weak she had become as she struggled against the hold around her waist, realizing she could not push him off.

"Don't fight, don't fucking fight."

Frantic, she fought harder, managing to shove him back enough to take a few steps before she was slammed against the wall again hard, a line of cold metal at her throat making her instantly numb.

"I told you not to fight, bitch."

She thought of Livvie, of Elena, of everything, and she had so much to live for, so much to make right, she wasn't going out like this.

"Where's your phone?" He shoved his hand roughly into the pockets of her jeans, groping her.

"It's in my jacket pocket." She gritted out the words, turning her head as he leaned in closer, feeling him retrieve the device before he squeezed each of her breasts appreciatively, hard. A new fear crawled sick into her chest.

"Pretty. Wish we had more time together, doll." He palmed her ass and she prayed the words meant he was going to leave. A car rolled by on the street and she sucked in a breath to scream, headlights passing the mouth of the alley, momentarily illuminating his face. He looked into the light and panic crossed his face, the knife pressing too hard against her neck in his distraction, before it was gone, he was gone, off and running into the darkness.

It took her a second to push away from the wall, to stagger forward exhausted and still terrified, and catch her bearings. Once she did, she set off running, and didn't stop until she was all the way home.

The knife had barely nicked her skin, leaving a single thin line about three inches across the left of her throat. It burned, but what burned more was the memory of his hands on her. She showered, hating that the mugger was the last person to touch her, like his presence there had somehow undone Elena's, making her feel even further from Elena now, absolutely lost.

She crawled into bed and tapped out a quick email on her laptop to Ruby, explaining she had been robbed and to please communicate with her through email until she got a new phone, and then fell into a deep, and thankfully dreamless, sleep.

Chapter Fourteen

She was falling asleep on the sofa, another workday over, another day of swimming against the current, through the fog. Realizing it would be selfish to let Winling worry, she had shot her a quick email, thinking more carefully about her wording now the panic of the previous night had worn off, telling her she had lost her phone and she was doing okay. She was sure there ought to be more people in her life she had to tell she was unreachable by phone—it was painful to realize there wasn't.

When the knocking started, she glanced at the clock and around her messy apartment. Nine-thirty was late, even for Winling. The knocking came again, and she swung open the door, ready to tell them to fuck off.

Elena stood there.

The sight of her knocked the breath out of Maya, shock, sadness, and a wave of hurt swallowing her.

She was trying to find something to say when Elena pushed past her, inviting herself in.

"You were *robbed*?"

Maya stood there uselessly in the doorway, still trying to process the fact that Elena was there, in her home. Elena grabbed her arm, pulled her forward, and closed the door behind her. Once it was done, she didn't let go, and the contact grounded her.

"Ruby called me. Were you hurt?" She was furious again, and Maya longed for a time when there was more between them than anger and sadness and that painful past tense.

She cleared her throat. "No... He just took my phone and um...just my phone."

"And what?"

Elena reached behind her and flicked on the light switch, hissing, the sound feral and feline as her eyes fell to the thin red line on Maya's throat.

"He cut you?"

"It's just a scratch, really..."

Soft fingers tracing the line messily killed the words in her mouth.

"Tell me exactly what happened."

There was no question in her tone, and somehow that made it easier for Maya to do as Elena asked.

"I was walking last night, and this man asked me for the time. I checked my phone, which in hindsight was stupid. He pushed me into an alley, I tried to fight, and then he pulled a knife. He took my phone and just...groped me a little bit." She swallowed hard. "And then he left."

"He touched you?" Her voice was murder.

Maya nodded.

"Where?"

Elena was dark and dangerous and brimming with righteous anger and perhaps a hint of possessiveness, or maybe that was what Maya wanted to believe. Childishly, she indicated her chest and her butt.

"Oh Maya." Elena's voice was soft, and it was like coming home, though it was full of a pity Maya couldn't take, couldn't let inside her for fear it would break her open. Finally, she pulled her arm out of Elena's grasp.

"I'm fine, it was hardly anything. I'm just glad it wasn't worse."

A somber silence hung over them, and she took a minute to study Elena. She looked exhausted, her tremor as bad as Maya had ever seen it, dark rings under her tired eyes.

"Did you report it?"

She shook her head and Elena opened her mouth, probably to berate her. Maya cut her off.

"Don't, please, just don't."

The silence between them was stony again as they hovered awkward in the hall, Elena looking dangerously unsteady.

"Would you like to sit?"

Maya followed her as she moved to the sofa and perched on the edge, watching as Elena scanned the space.

"You're so thin, sweetheart."

The endearment almost broke her, and she grit her teeth against its weight. Elena seemed surprised by her own words, and Maya heard her swallow hard.

"Were you seeing him all along?"

The question was soft, broken, and sincere like Elena could seriously believe it might be true, and God, the thought infuriated Maya.

"Please tell me you're joking?"

Her disbelief seemed to offend Elena, and Maya watched her straighten her spine, a hardness entering her eyes.

"Do I look like I'm joking? Is it an unreasonable assumption that two people French kissing in the middle of a dance floor might have been...intimate over a period of time?"

Maya wondered if she really thought so little of her.

"There was no two people, Elena. Kevin kissed me. I was wasted and angry and I took way too long to shove him off, but I never kissed him back. I never wanted him to do that. I don't know if you noticed but I've been in love with you for almost a year now, only you."

She threw up her hands. Elena laughed, dark and hard, the sound making Maya's heart sink.

"Well, that wasn't how it looked when you were dancing with that little bull dyke from the seventh floor, or when you stood there with your eyes closed while Kevin James shoved his tongue in your mouth."

"I told you—" She started but she never got to finish, Elena was white-hot and angry, and Maya was standing in the heat of her flames, gloriously burning, her presence worth the fight.

"Don't! Don't you fucking dare. Do you have any idea how you made me look? Do you know what my mother said to me the next day?" She laughed, a hollow sound. "She told me that of course you didn't love me, of course you didn't want to raise a child with me. She said no one ever would, unless it was someone like Robin who could see the value of my lineage, someone worldly enough to look past my *shortcomings*. She told me she hoped I could see you for the gold-digging little tramp you are."

"I have never, once, asked you for money." Maya's tone was dark. She saw the sick smile that twisted onto Elena's face and knew Elena wanted to fight. She didn't know if she had the strength to oblige.

"So, if it wasn't my money, then what?" Elena spat the words. "Were you just so desperate for attention you chose the first person who paused to look at you? Poor desperate, disabled Elena would want you, right?"

Hurt and anger were a potent cocktail in Maya's blood, but before she could interject Elena was speaking again.

"Or perhaps it's those pesky mommy issues. Poor little orphan Maya looking for someone to belong to. Is that why you like it rough?"

Maya swung back to slap her again, and Elena messily blocked the blow with her arm, surprising them both.

"Oops, did I hit a nerve?" Her voice was changing, evolving, spilling into something dark that Maya loved and loathed in equal measure. "Is that what I was for you, someone brave enough to treat you like the broken little girl you really are?"

It was a delicate subject. Maya had still been coming to terms with herself, with the fact that she did enjoy power play with Elena, that she liked to be dominated in a way she hadn't expected, and hearing it laid out so crassly was humiliating. Hot tears of shame pricked the back of her eyes.

"Do you think Kevin James would love you like I did, Maya? Do you think he would treat you like a princess, and like a dirty little *whore*?"

Tears spilled down her cheeks. She wanted to run and at the same time she didn't want it to end. She shook her head.

"Use your words." Elena commanded her, their relationship slipping back into something familiar, and just like that, Maya was conquered.

"No."

Elena's dark eyes were melting, their hardness slipping away as they became darker still, molten.

Maya hated this and she needed it, she desperately needed a line of communication, some way to work through things with Elena when everything between them felt so broken. This was the last thing she expected but clung to it like a lifeline.

"You're mine." There was no uncertainty in her tone, her jerking hands moving from where they had been gripping her knees to remain still to cup Maya's face.

Maya stared back, defiant for a few seconds, before she let herself go, let go of the guilt and the shame she felt and embraced what she wanted: Elena.

"I'm yours." She whispered the words. "I only ever wanted to be yours."

Elena seemed to soften, brushing her thumbs across Maya's cheeks, drying them, before her hands fell away.

"I'm sorry, I shouldn't have. You were attacked last night, and if Kevin really did assault you..."

Hearing those words, things were hard again, sharp shards and broken pieces littering the rapidly growing divide between them, and Maya ached to have the simplicity they had found a few moments ago returned.

"No, Elena, it was nothing like that. Please." The words came out hurried and her cheeks were hot under the dampness of her tears. "I want you, please, please. I'm yours, keep me, please."

A million insecurities came rushing to the surface, choking her, but she was rewarded with a sharp breath.

Elena's fingers closed around her throat and she surged forward and kissed her hard, her grip looser than she expected, hoped, and Maya wondered if today was one of her bad days with her symptoms.

"I'm sorry." She was crying again, and Elena's mouth covered hers, quieting her, her tongue forcing itself insistent into her mouth, reclaiming her.

"Do you want me just to hold you, sweetheart?" Elena pulled back to kiss her ear gently and look into her teary eyes.

Maya shook her head.

"Please, baby, touch me. I need you; we need this. Let go, please?"

Her eyes went dark with the plea, and Maya knew she had won.

Elena stripped her of her clothes with insistent hands until she was sitting naked on her couch, Elena inspecting her shamelessly.

"You're too thin."

Maya wasn't sure if she was supposed to apologize, embarrassed by the state of her body, the soft stubble that had grown between her legs in the time since Elena had left her.

"You're mine, darling, always, no matter what." Elena's voice was liquid, spilling hot and dangerous into her ear, her body pressed up against Maya's side, shaking hard. "And you must take care of yourself, always. Promise me."

Maya wasn't sure she could meet the demand. Elena's hand roamed over her breast, bringing her nipple to a fast peak before it was tweaked, hard.

"Promise me, sweetheart."

Pleasure and pain had her breathing faster, and feeling tears rising in her throat she shook her head, looking up at Elena through wet lashes.

"I can't..." She whispered the words. "You'll have to stay around and take care of me yourself."

Elena's eyes shone as she slid one hand up her neck, under her chin, and around into her hair until her head was yanked back.

"I think we both have some making up to do."

Maya tried to nod but the hand in her hair held her still, though she knew she could easily break the hold; she knew Elena was tired.

"Let me go first?" She asked the question innocently, wet eyes and her thin lip between her bottom teeth, her tangled hair cascading over her shoulders where it spilled from Elena's fist. When Elena tipped her head and released her from her grip, Maya scrambled down from the sofa. She removed Elena's jeans, dragging them down her trembling legs before boldly she leaned up and kissed her.

"I missed you so much."

Elena held her tight, kissing her again.

"I missed you, too, my love."

The sweet moment warmed Maya's heart, lightening the weight that had hung around her neck since the day of the party, and she was floating pleasantly yet totally grounded as she helped Elena raise her hips and wrestled her panties down her legs.

"I love you so much." She didn't give her time to reply, sinking back to her knees and fastening her mouth over her hot flesh, already pleasantly wet for her. Elena's moans sounded like the Hallelujah chorus, and Maya held her jerking hips down as best she could, as she messily licked her way over her, around her, inside her. She was eager to pleasure Elena, to let her lie back and enjoy herself, sensing how tired she was, knowing how weak she probably felt. Maya just wanted to worship her, to make her feel good, and she did.

Elena's slim hips bumped against her face, rutting, as Elena whined out her name, breathy and broken with her second orgasm, and Maya was lost, already chasing a third when she was pulled back by the roots of her hair, gently.

Elena looked down at her with hazy eyes.

"You're amazing, sweetheart."

The praise filled her up in a way she had finally stopped questioning.

"Come here." Elena summoned her and she went easily, her sex throbbing painfully, eager to be touched.

"Undress me, Maya."

She did, carefully pulling Elena's shirt over her head and making quick work of the bra she knew Elena would struggle with. When Elena was naked before her, she waited, expectant.

"Take me to bed."

She did, pulling Elena to her feet and hanging on her arm as they walked to the room, watching as Elena flicked on the soft lamp and moved to lie on her unmade bed. She patted the spot beside her, and Maya went willingly. She lay on her back, looking up into hungry eyes. Her legs were patted apart, and she opened them obediently.

"Are you wet for me, darling?"

She nodded, earning her a dark look, prompting her to quickly correct herself.

"Yes."

Elena was rubbing a firm palm up and down her abdomen, brushing the fuzz between her legs and then travelling back up to squeeze her breasts. Maya's hips were already grinding into the mattress.

"Rub yourself for me."

It took her a few seconds to process the request. Brushing away her embarrassment, Maya reached down and ran two fingers over her sensitive flesh, the feeling making her draw in a breath.

Apparently pleased, Elena leaned down to kiss her. Maya was besotted with the way she could so easily control her, own her, set her alight and burn her in the most wonderful way, even when she was physically not at her strongest.

"Does it feel good, sweetheart?"

"Mm... Yes, but I want you." She was shameless in her need now. Elena's lips and teeth and tongue in her mouth, on her neck, over her collarbones and nipples were nice, but it was not enough.

"Fuck me, baby."

Elena purred in response.

"My greedy girl."

A hot tongue slicked up the side of her neck, replaced by teeth and a rough suction, Elena leaving her mark as she slipped a finger inside, making Maya yelp.

"I'm the only one who gets to touch you like this."

Maya nodded her agreement, her hips already riding Elena's hand hard, the memory of watching Elena's previous orgasm leaving her tantalizingly close already.

"You're all mine, Miss Scott. I am never letting you go again."

A second finger shoved into her, and Maya's mouth fell open, panting out her pleasure as Elena pushed her higher and higher, closer.

"I'm going to take better care of you, darling. I won't ever let you feel like you're less."

Maya moaned uselessly. A million things she wanted to say, promises she wanted to make, dissolved as Elena twisted her fingers inside her, her own still rubbing a frantic pace over her clit.

"You're going to gain some weight, and there'll be no more wandering around at night, and I'm going to make you so fucking happy, Maya Scott."

She was vicious in her conviction. Her words, the things Elena was doing to her body, had her spinning into euphoria, and Maya's orgasm was coming, closer, closer.

"My precious girl, I love you so...fucking...much." She punctuated the last three words with three rough thrusts inside her and Maya felt herself go careening over the edge. Her moan of pleasure turned to an outraged scream when Elena's fingers were abruptly pulled out of her and her own hand was yanked off her clit and pinned to the bed.

She looked down helplessly as her orgasm slipped away, leaving frustrated tears in her eyes.

"And you're going to promise me a few things too."

Elena was smirking down at her, and Maya should have known there would be one final play in her book.

"You're going to take better care of yourself, Miss Scott. No matter what happens you are valuable, and you have your daughter to think of too. You're going to promise to try harder to communicate with me, which includes keeping your phone on and not running away if we have a fight. I will do the same. And lastly, you're going to promise me that you will strive to never, ever let anyone in this world make you feel less, me included because, darling, you are enough, a million times enough and so much more."

The tears of frustration became tears of emotion.

"I promise."

Elena smiled.

"Now, promise me that you're mine, then I'm going to fuck your brains out."

Something deep in Maya's stomach clenched at the words alone.

"I promise."

With a tender kiss that ended in a wicked smile, Elena moved down the mattress, two fingers rough inside her and a hot mouth all over her when she came for the first time of many, that night.

*

Maya woke to the late summer sun filtering softly through her window, turning Elena's ebony hair to copper in its light. She was suddenly scared, terrified that the cold light of day would break the fragile forgiveness they had found the previous night. Maya was sure sex was not the answer to every problem, but somehow, in their own way, through their unique relationship, they had been able to work through things using it as a vessel. Elena was warm against her under the covers, and she savored the moment, unwilling to waste another second with her.

"I can feel you staring."

Elena's voice was rough with sleep, and badly slurred. As she moved to sit up, she struggled to push herself back onto the pillows. Maya helped her, pleased that the time when the action might have offended Elena had passed.

"I just love you." She tested the words out, pleased when a brilliant smile lit tired features, and Elena reached for her hand. She missed once before she was able to grab it.

"I love you too. We'll figure everything out."

The words warmed Maya from the inside out.

"Is today a bad day?"

Elena knew what she meant instantly.

"The last few days have all been...hard, and unfortunately when I came over last night after hearing that you were robbed from Ruby—we are going to talk about that later by the way—I didn't bring a bag, nor my medicine."

Her words were slow, and she seemed to struggle over them in a way Maya rarely heard.

"Go back to bed, baby. Let me go get your meds and maybe pack a bag for you?" She made the offer carefully, hoping Elena felt as she did and wanted to spend the weekend together.

"You're so good to me." Soft lips kissed hers and then Elena slumped back down onto the pillows.

"My house keys are in my pants pocket, wherever they may be."

There was a smile in her voice that Maya felt reflected in her heart as she pushed herself out of bed and dressed slowly.

"And Miss Scott?"

Maya turned to look at her.

"Hurry back."

*

Maya floated through the drive to Elena's house, finally awake, finally living, breathing after weeks of torturous stasis. The future still hung heavy on her mind, the looming court date still haunted her, and she missed her daughter so much it was a physical ache, but somehow, it was less daunting now Elena was back in her world.

Stepping back into the mansion, not realizing how much she had missed the place, it hit her hard. The place was spotless, as always, everything exactly how she remembered it, and her heart fell for a second. Outwardly it looked as if Elena had kept her life together much better than Maya had during their separation. She told herself not to read into that and moved quickly through the familiar space, room after room, until she reached Elena's bedroom.

She slipped into the bathroom and opened the medicine cabinet above the sink as she had seen Elena do so many times, though she had never actually looked inside.

In her head she had expected to find a single prescription pill bottle, the one Elena always took a pill from every morning when she had watched her morning routine with lazy eyes. Instead, she was greeted by several prescription bottles, a host of over the counter medicines from painkillers to cough suppressors, muscle rub, muscle patches, and two different sizes of heating pads. Not for the first time, she marveled at Elena's strength, that this was what she had to keep in her arsenal to deal with her daily life, and Maya had no idea.

She read off a few of the pill bottles, unsure which was the magic one Elena usually used. Four times a day daily, twice a day daily, three times a day daily, as needed, no more than six in twenty-four hours... How many pills did Elena take per day? How much did she really struggle with her condition? How many times had she fallen here alone with no one to help her up? Questions haunted Maya as she retrieved Elena's overnight bag from the closet and swiped the entire two shelves of medications into it.

Elena was always so strong that it was easy to overlook the battle she fought daily, and Maya resolved to do better, to support her more, to care for her, to try to take some of the weight. Suddenly she was eager to get back to her apartment and get through the talk she knew they needed to have that morning, to get back to normalcy. She plucked some clothes from the closet, enough for the weekend, and feeling hopeful, an outfit for work on Monday. She grabbed Elena's makeup and, on a whim, slid open the drawer beside her bed and chunked the toy inside into the bag too.

Before she could slide it closed, the shine of something metal caught her eye, and peering down into its corner, she caught sight of a wedding ring set with stones so large she wondered if the diamonds could even be real. Perhaps it was Elena's grandmother's, or her mother's from a previous marriage. She closed the drawer and stopped by the kitchen to grab a bottle of water for the ride home.

Something sticking out the top of the trash can made her pause, slung there messily in a way that was very unlike Elena and out of place with the rest of her pristine home, shoved rapidly inside and not pushed down. Taking a long drink, she set down the overnight bag and retrieved the book from atop the empty boxes and vegetable peelings in the trash can.

Mind the Step—Becoming a Stepparent.

Maya's heart jumped in her chest. Beneath the book was another, *My Partner's Toddler.* Maya set both books on the counter and dug out the balled-up papers below them, some part of her brain aware that she was prying, crossing a line that maybe she shouldn't, but they were already in her hands and she was smoothing them down on the counter beside the books.

She pored over page after page of developmental milestones for three-year-olds, educational play ideas, and all the different skills parents should be trying to teach at home for this age group. Tears pricked her eyes. Elena had made notes in the margins, her large shaky handwriting littered with accidental pen strokes and smudges.

A category beside the milestone list had been added to say "Livvie," and next to each item—*speak clearly, speak in five to six word sentences*—and so on, Elena had added a check mark, and in some cases written "advanced" too. Maya's heart swelled with love for Elena, tears thick in her throat, because something this good just didn't happen for her.

She wasn't the messed-up bumbling through life twenty-three-year-old who was somehow noticed by a gorgeous older woman and wanted. She wasn't the one the amazing woman decided to keep, and then also fell in love with her kid too. Happily ever afters like the one staring her in the face just didn't happen for her, but looking down at Elena's research, her notes, the evidence of time, and lots of it, spent for Livvie's benefit, Maya felt like they might.

She smoothed the papers lovingly, placed them on top of the books in the middle of the counter, and slung the bag over her shoulder, and then she headed for the door. When she opened it, she jumped in surprise, painfully aware of her still sex-ruined hair pulled into a messy bun, and her yoga pants and hoodie attire.

She recognized the woman who had accompanied Elena to the party, the one Elena had said was called Robin, ascending the steps to the front door. Robin stopped short at the sight of Maya, who was in the process of turning the key in the lock.

"I didn't expect to see you still here, and with a key too... Elena must be wealthier than I thought. She clearly doesn't care about getting robbed."

Robin reminded Maya of what she imagined a young Cara Mars would be like, all the entitlement, the condescending untouchable attitude, before she learned to behave in public, before she got clever enough to display those undesirable traits in an underhanded way instead.

"Elena's not home." Maya grit her teeth and ground out the words. All of this had started because she was childish, and as much as she hated the pomp and circumstance, all the games, for better or for worse, this was Elena's world, and she wanted to do better, to prove she could if not necessarily belong there, at least navigate it gracefully for Elena's sake.

"That's a shame. I was hoping for a nice cooked breakfast and back to bed for dessert. Elena's fairly useless as far as most things go but damn, can she cook. She is a little quiet in the sack for my tastes though."

Maya's blood boiled and she was reminded of her time in the group homes. There were always bigger kids, stronger kids, taunting her, bullying her, yet she had never quite learned to bite her tongue no matter how hard she'd tried, and she'd taken the beatings for it. She had to do better about controlling herself now.

"Look, Robin is it?"

Robin nodded, all short platinum hair and an expensive black overcoat.

"Elena can speak for herself, so if you want something from her—breakfast, sex, whatever it is—you'll have to ask her. But please, don't speak about my girlfriend like that. Elena's not useless, she's amazing, and frankly better than all of us, you and me included."

The words were diplomatic and quite grown up. Maya was proud of herself for the response. Robin laughed.

"My, you are good. I can see why you've got her fooled, but tell me, just between us, Maya, it's the money, right?"

Maya caught her left hand balled tight in a fist and shook it out at her side. She was not going to deck this woman, she wasn't.

"I mean, Elena's a good-looking woman but you just can't really enjoy it, you know? All that shaking, the jerking, the weird speech... I heard she drooled while giving a talk at the Venetian last year."

Robin laughed, a cruel sound, cold, mocking, mean in a way that invaded Maya's ears and sank down into her bones, her muscles, pulling them tight. Again, she fought the urge to hit her.

"I mean if you're into that, okay, but then what does she even see in you? Sure, you're younger, you were attractive enough at the party in a trashy one-night kind of way, but Cara says you have a kid you lost, Robert Holt's daughter? College dropout, and you work for her? I'm sure Elena knows her limitations and knows she needs to find someone who'll stick around for her despite the...you know." She raised her arms, shaking spastically in a cruel imitation of Elena, and Maya reeled back, barely, barely catching herself before she socked Robin in the face.

Robin went on, "But surely she knows with as much money as she has, she can do a little better than you? I for one could deal with her for her trust fund alone, never mind what she makes. I draw the line at kids though. Having a retarded wife would be bad enough without having a kid to match."

Maya punched her.

It was a blazing left hook that made her knuckles burn, the force of it throwing her off balance and sending her toppling down the stairs, her cheek bumping painfully against the edge of a concrete step as she fell. As she rolled to her feet, her fists were already up. Elena's bag jostled, no worse for wear at her side, as her history told her to expect retaliation.

Robin was bent over, one hand clinging to the rail, holding her bloody nose. When Maya wiped at her throbbing cheek, her fingers came back stained with blood.

"You assaulted me!"

Robin was literally crying, tears streaming down her face, whether from the shock of being hit or the blow to her nose, Maya wasn't sure.

"Sure did."

Somewhere deep down she panicked, remembering she was supposed to do better, to be better, and also acutely aware of how this would look for her approaching court date.

Robin was still bent over uselessly on the steps fingering her busted face, and Maya had a plan.

"Here's what's going to happen. You're going to disappear out of Elena's life, or don't actually, I don't care, but you will never, ever use that word to describe her, or anyone, again."

She stepped up one step, all bluff and bravado, the terrified blue eyes peering up at her from above Robin's bloody hand making her brave.

"Here's the thing about someone like me, Robin. We know people, people who don't care about money, or fancy parties, or the price tag on your shoes. I met people in prison, people you don't want to see even in your nightmares, and those people owe me. So you're going to speak respectfully about Elena, and you're going to tell anyone who asks that you took a tumble down these little steps here and busted your nose, and we're going to go our separate ways and I won't bother sending my friends to pay you a visit. Sound good?"

She nodded, and Maya almost laughed. Unable to resist, she pressed a finger to her lips, to indicate silence, cackling wickedly on the inside as Robin copied, pressing a bloody finger to her stained lips in response and nodding frantically to indicate that she understood.

*

"You *punched* her?"

Elena was sitting up in bed, rummaging through her overnight bag and checking the label on bottle after bottle in search of the pills she needed.

"I'm sorry, baby!" Maya's voice was a whine, and the words were only half true.

"What on Earth did she say to you?"

Maya refused to repeat the term; she refused to speak it again and give something so ugly more air time, and most of all, she refused to cast Robin's hateful words on Elena and risk them tarnishing her even for a second.

"She was just talking down to me, patronizing me."

"I'm sorry, darling, but it's still not a good reason to hit her. What about the court date? I don't know if she would bother to report it, but if she does, Maya, it could impact the decision about Livvie."

Elena looked terrified, and while Maya worried over it, too, she was pretty sure she had scared Robin good enough that she would keep her mouth shut.

"We came to an agreement. She isn't going to tell anyone."

"You came to an agreement?" Elena repeated the words disbelievingly.

"Okay, so I very maturely threatened to sic my prison buddies on her if she talked and she damn near peed her pants."

Elena snorted with laughter.

"Yes, very mature, Miss Scott."

Maya took a fake little bow and moved to sit on the edge of the bed. She stuck out her tongue at Elena, who just rolled her eyes, finally victorious in organizing her meds.

"She did say something that made me curious... This isn't why I hit her, by the way."

Elena took the bottle of water from the nightstand. She struggled with the cap before Maya took it from her, opened it, and passed it back, ignoring the liquid that sloshed over the rim and soaked the bedsheets as Elena raised it to her mouth to swallow her pills.

"She said you two had slept together."

Elena wiped her mouth.

"We have."

"Oh." Her words somehow captured her exact feelings in the moment and Elena rolled her eyes.

"Not recently, and I have no plans to do so again. Don't look so dejected, Miss Scott, you weren't exactly a virgin when we met either."

Maya tried to look unbothered. She knew the information irked her out of habit, rather than real insecurity now. Robin was someone she perhaps would have thought to be better for Elena, once upon a time, but if anything, their run-in that morning had proven to Maya that while she was not as wealthy and undoubtedly at a financial disadvantage to Elena's rich friends and family, she was infinitely wealthier and more fortunate in other ways.

"She said you were too quiet in bed. Which seemed strange. I mean, did you not, um—"

God, she was still too embarrassed to say the word, and what even was the word? Was there a name for the way Elena took control of her so effortlessly?

"Power play wasn't a part of our sex life."

Oh.

"That is something I enjoy uniquely with you."

"So, you've never done that before? I thought you had... I mean, me either but you just seem so—"

Elena cut her off.

"I have, but the roles were always reversed." She gave Maya a sinful smile. "I find I like it this way quite a bit better though."

Damn this woman and her ability to still make her blush.

"Do you ever miss being—?"

She was a blundering mumbling mess and she wondered if she would ever get used to this, ever finish coming to terms with the fact she liked this, that she was...kinky?

"On the bottom?"

The words sounded decadent on Elena's tongue, and she nodded, telling herself to chill. They at least needed to shower and wash off the remnants of last night's marathon before they got into that all over again.

"Not at all, I like how we are together. Previously such encounters had felt like a roleplay, in the sense I was playing the role someone else wanted of me. With you, I feel honestly, unapologetically, like I can be myself."

Maya marveled at how eloquent she was on the subject.

"Me too."

Her reply earned her a smile, before Elena changed the topic.

"I suppose we need to talk about everything that happened."

Maya nodded.

"It all seems so stupid now, though, doesn't it?"

They both laughed, relief evident in the sound before the room fell silent, the pause pregnant. Elena spoke first.

"Before we talk about us, I did want to talk about you getting mugged."

Maya groaned inwardly. She had almost forgotten the incident entirely, too busy with her relief, her absolute joy that, somehow, it seemed she and Elena would be able to reconcile.

"I know you don't want to talk about it."

"I don't, really, I'm fine." She gave her the best smile she could manage, hoping it would be enough to get her to drop it. "I was no big deal, Elena, really."

"Perhaps." Her eyes were too dark, and Maya knew she had more to say. "It wasn't a big deal for you, but from what you told me it could have been. You were lucky, the next woman he corners might not be."

The thought made her blood run cold, the memory of the fear, the disgust rising in her throat to choke her.

Elena's shaking hand held hers tight.

"I don't want to upset you. I just think you should report it. It shouldn't take long and even giving a description could help save someone else from experiencing what you did, or worse."

She was right and Maya nodded.

"I'll make a call on Monday."

Elena reached up to touch her cheek, caressing her softly with jerking fingers.

"If you want to talk about it, I'm always here, and I always want to listen."

She nodded, but honestly, she didn't.

"Thanks." She cleared her throat. "So, about everything...us."

Elena's eyes lingered on her face for a second longer. What she was looking for Maya didn't know but, apparently satisfied, Elena let her hand fall away. The tension in the room doubled, changing tangibly, and she knew they had switched tracks.

Silence hung around them, and she was looking for a way to open, a place to begin, trying to find the words to start, when Elena took a deep breath.

"I'm so sorry I ever agreed to go to the stupid party with her. I had my reasons, but I understand now how it must have looked to you, how you must have felt. I'm so angry that I made you feel unimportant, sweetheart."

Maya swallowed the lump in her throat because it had, but it didn't excuse her actions afterward.

"I'm sorry I acted like such a child, not answering my phone and trying to get under your skin at the party, and for not pushing Kevin off sooner, though honestly that wasn't intentional at all."

"That wasn't your fault. I see that now. I'm sorry it took me so long to realize."

"But still, I'm sorry you were embarrassed in front of your parents and I know it hurt you. Thank you for not firing me totally, by the way."

The words poured out and she sucked in a big breath, trying not to remember her first day on the fourth floor, all the nights after, that had just bled into one big blur of misery to her now.

"I don't think anything has ever hurt me more than that day in the stairwell," Elena confessed. She reached for her and Maya went willingly, allowing herself to be guided into her lap. Elena's shaking arms wrapped around her and held her tight. She breathed her in and exhaled some of the stress of the past few weeks.

"I was having a panic attack, I think," she supplied, embarrassed.

"You were, and it took everything in me not to just dry your tears and take you back and offer to share you with Kevin."

Maya opened her mouth to protest but Elena shushed her.

"I was in a bad place and hadn't realized the errors in my assumptions at that point. I thought perhaps you'd been seeing him all along behind my back. It hadn't occurred to me that it was just a mistake on his part."

Maya nodded, a new line of thought piquing her interest.

"Would you—share me, I mean? With someone else, obviously not him."

Elena kissed her temple and considered the question, and Maya loved her for her openness, for the easy dialogue between them, for the fact they could talk about this.

"I have dabbled in polyamory, and while I understand that it's foolish to think you can be absolutely everything to one person, to assume the fact that they love someone else too means they love you any less, I don't think I could share you."

Maya's heart was soaring, though Elena's voice was apologetic.

"If you wanted that, I would...try." The word in itself seemed like a strain.

"You are just so... I feel so strongly for you, I have since the day we met. I get possessive and crazy and the thought of someone else getting to be with you is difficult for me... But if your happiness depended on it—"

"It doesn't." Maya cut her off. She loved hearing her work through it, getting a glimpse inside the way her mind operated, but she couldn't listen to Elena torturing herself over the idea anymore. "I'm not interested in that, not at all... I only want you."

They shared a sweet kiss, a beat passing before it began to turn deeper, darker.

"We need to shower." Maya was loath to interrupt where she felt they were headed but it was true. She couldn't help but wonder about Elena's past, her being so much more experienced in many things. She almost asked her about it, but ultimately decided against bringing up anything that could ruin their very pleasant reunion.

"To be continued then?"

Maya nodded and crawled off the bed. She helped Elena to her feet, holding her hand to steady her until she had her balance. Stripping off her clothes, she watched her disappear, smooth tan thighs topped by a deliciously round ass, and she wondered if perhaps they ought to combine the plan of continuing where that kiss had been headed with the plan to shower.

As she hurried to join Elena in the bathroom, she tripped over a stuffed animal, the joy bleeding out of her moment, replaced by the ache of missing Livvie, the worry over the fast approaching custody hearing, though it reminded her of something, which helped her breathe.

Elena was already sitting in the tub, the water filling around her.

"While I was at your place, before Robin, I was getting a drink and I um, I saw the books in the trash."

Rouge colored Elena's cheeks and Maya continued talking, eager to make her understand quickly, hating for her to be embarrassed over something that was so amazing to her.

"Elena, I was blown away. The fact you care enough to buy a book and read it is amazing. You don't see Livvie as an inconvenience or an add-on, you actually...love her?"

It became a question and Elena nodded vehemently. "I do, of course I do. How on earth could I not?"

Maya's heart swelled as she leaned on the doorframe.

"You and I, we're in good shape, right? I mean we're pretty permanent?"

"I hope so."

Nodding, Maya wet her lips, suddenly nervous.

"I don't know if I'll win the custody hearing, but if I do, I'll be raising Livvie, and you're my girlfriend, and I want you to be part of her life, Elena. I want you to help raise her... For us to raise her together—if you want to?"

Elena was nodding, tears springing into her eyes, and Maya crossed the space quickly and bent at the edge of the tub to kiss her.

"I do want that."

Maya squeezed a shaky hand hard, smiling through her own tears as she looked at her, determined to remember this moment forever.

"Okay."

Chapter Fifteen

After a weekend spent blissfully reconnecting with Elena, Maya was sick with nerves when it finally came to an end. Although she was promptly reinstated at her old desk first thing Monday morning, the custody hearing on Thursday was approaching fast, with the winter benefit right behind it on Friday night.

The office was a madhouse, everyone racing to meet deadlines and apply finishing touches to the seating plan, the entertainment schedule, the catering. She was grateful for the distraction it created, and that she was thrown right back into working, leaving little time for gossip and questions from her coworkers.

Kathryn and Margaret greeted her with hugs and kind words about how she was missed. Even Dave stopped quickly to thank her for coming back, reminding her that more than just her coworkers, these people were her friends.

Kevin was particularly stony, though she put it down to bruised male pride and ignored him for the most part. His behavior did make her wonder if she had been wrong to ask Elena not to fire him. Elena had been absolutely furious while she had explained originally that she planned to let him go after realizing the kiss was not consensual. Maya didn't know if it was her own insecurity, but she couldn't help but feel guilty. She hadn't pushed him away, and as soon as she did, he had stopped. As much as she hated what had happened, she didn't want him to lose his job over it, even though his presence now made her uncomfortable.

Over lunch she and Elena met with Ruby and her wife Peyton, who Maya instantly loved. They went over documents and practice questions and made sure they were fully prepared for Thursday, and as nervous as she felt, Maya knew she was ready.

Ruby was kind but confident, clear in her instructions but supportive as well, and Maya was so ridiculously grateful that they had her on their side.

Elena had held her hand the entire time, and just her supportive presence gave Maya hope. Somehow with Elena beside her, and Ruby representing her, she felt like maybe, just maybe, she could win.

As they reentered the office, the large metal doors clicking closed on the elevator behind them, Elena caught her by the hem of her jacket and pulled her back as she moved to head to her desk. Maya barely had time to wonder what she needed before Elena was planting a lingering kiss right on her mouth. Her heart stopped, acutely aware of the rest of the staff in the space before them, but even in her shocked state she couldn't help but kiss Elena back, part of her loving finally laying claim to the woman publicly.

"They all know anyway so I decided I wouldn't deny myself."

With that wicked grin still on her lips she headed over to Margaret's desk, no doubt to coordinate with her before they attacked the afternoon's workload. With her cheeks burning, Maya headed for her own desk, grimacing as Kevin's cool eyes followed her.

"So, it's true then, love?"

Of course, he was speaking to her now, sitting at his desk with Kathryn and Adam hovering close by as they finished their lunch break.

"Yes, I'm dating Elena, as I said last week."

Kathryn squealed.

"Oh my God, Maya! That's amazing, you two are adorable together. Since when?"

Before she could answer Kevin laughed loudly.

"Wow...Scott, didn't peg you as the type to fuck your way to the top. Can I even call it that? Well, finger then. Either way I am surprised."

"Seriously, man, come on."

Adam interrupted on her behalf and Maya shot him a grateful glance.

Kevin held his hands up, seemingly chastised though he continued to run his mouth.

"Just makes me wonder. And I also wonder what the old man of that little girl of yours thinks about you trying to make Elena her new daddy? Can't be good for the kid being raised like that."

Her heart was falling, the elation of their preparation at lunch, the butterflies that still lingered from the kiss all dropping away and leaving only anger in their wake. She was about to finally open her mouth and let all the things she had held back all year tumble out, her politeness worn out by his constant snide remarks and derogatory comments, but someone else spoke first.

"Mr. James."

Elena's voice was thunder, so loud that Kevin jumped visibly in his seat as she interrupted, appearing behind him so quickly even Maya hadn't noticed her there.

"Pack your shit."

Every word was enunciated perfectly. Maya's jaw dropped, but some of the weight she hadn't even realized she had carried since the kiss incident left her chest.

"You're fired."

He didn't leave gracefully, but thankfully, after security came up to escort him out, he did leave. In a surprising show of solidarity, it had been Adam and Kathryn who finally said what everyone was thinking and told him to shut up as he insulted Elena loudly while packing up his desk.

Watching Kathryn share a smile with her and seeing Adam with his hand on Elena's shoulder while he asked her if she was okay, Maya had never felt more at home at a job than she did at TMF.

Once the uproar of Kevin's departure died down, the rest of the day was a blur of fielding phone calls, answering emails, and trying to pretend she wasn't texting Winling a very detailed recounting of his epic dismissal under the table, *PACK YOUR SHIT!!!!!* becoming her new favorite phrase.

*

Elena blew into the office like a storm after lunch on Tuesday. The anxiety that had taken up permanent residence in Maya's chest gave way to a more pressing concern, as thoughts of the court hearing were momentarily banished by the dark look on her girlfriend's face.

She watched, curious, as Elena headed toward Margaret's desk and then seemed to change her mind, stopping before she arrived and turning instead to address the room.

"If I could have your attention, please."

She didn't have to ask twice, the office falling eerily silent at her behest.

"Due to issues with our higher-ups"—she ground out the words—"the funding that was to be provided by The Mars Foundation for the winter benefit has been withdrawn."

The hum of voices rose around the room, everyone uncertain in the face of this huge announcement. They had been working on the benefit since the start of the year: since Maya had started with the company. Losing the funding was a huge blow, and Maya could only imagine the level of stress Elena was under right now. Guilt trickled hot into her stomach, because she had a feeling the funding had been pulled in part due to events inspired by her.

When the room quieted again, she watched Elena turn to Margaret.

"Factoring in the sponsorships and donations, how much of a deficit are we looking at with the Foundation unable to make a contribution?"

Margaret tapped away on a calculator at her desk and the office held its breath. It was going to be a huge amount. The entertainment was varied and fun, and having worked some on the bookings Maya knew those would be thousands alone, plus the cost of food, the bar, the venue... There was no way they were going to be able to raise the money for the event to go ahead in such a short time.

"Twenty-seven thousand dollars give or take. A little more once we finalize the entertainment and rentals." Elena's lips were fixed in a grim line. "We are in somewhat of a crisis, but I am by no means giving up. We have all worked too hard, and the charities we plan to help with the proceeds from the evening are far too deserving, but I wanted to keep all of you in the loop honestly with the situation as it stands." She swayed on her feet, her voice easily projecting around the room, her words clear in a way that Maya knew took much effort on her part. "For now, please continue working, and I will work on a solution."

She disappeared back into her office, whispers escalating into worried chatter as she went. Margaret shared a concerned look with Maya from across the room, to which she gave her a sad smile in reply, before pushing up from her desk and making her way down the hall to Elena's office.

The door was half closed, Elena sitting at her desk with her head in her hands, staring down at a typed page.

"Elena?"

She looked up, though the token smile she offered didn't reach her eyes.

"What happened?"

Maya had a sinking feeling she already knew.

"My mother. She's punishing me, and in her twisted mind it doesn't matter if hundreds of innocent children suffer through her actions, as long as I get what she sees as my comeuppance."

"For dating me?"

She nodded glumly.

"Among other things, yes, but darling, this is no reflection on you and it's not your fault. It's mine. I let my mother control my life for far too long, and as such she feels she's entitled to do something like this when, finally, I start living for myself."

The words only partially soothed the burn.

"She's also mad that I fired Kevin, but I absolutely draw the line at him bringing our...Livvie into this."

Maya's heart beat hard as she tried not to imagine the way the sentence was originally supposed to end. Was Elena about to refer to Livvie as their daughter? The question opened a whole world of want inside her, glimpses of a future that felt so strangely within reach yet was still so vastly unattainable. The idea swallowed her, taking her out of the present until the scratching of Elena's pen rough across the page brought her back. Focusing herself on the crisis at hand, she pushed on.

"What are we going to do? Twenty-seven thousand is a huge amount of money and the benefit is in three days. There's no way we can come up with it in time. Right?"

She ran her fingers through her hair, tugging on the blonde strands, trying to elicit a helpful thought, a plan, an idea.

"I think..." Elena first looked thoughtful and then startlingly resolute. "I think I'll fund the rest personally."

The sun came out across her face, and her smile was absolutely dazzling.

"My house is paid for, I make enough money to live well, and have even more saved, plenty to send Livvie to college and we still won't have to worry. I'm in a position to be able to do this, and that's a gift, right?"

She was so excited, Maya was once again knocked off her feet by Elena's wealth, and by the long-term future she so easily seemed to be planning for them together. She knew Elena was well off, but the fact sort of faded into background, meaning every time it was yanked forward in such stark relief, she was almost surprised by it all over again.

"That would be, I mean... Elena, that's amazing, and generous, and wow—"

"If all those children stood to lose everything they could gain from the proceeds of this benefit, and to prevent that all you had to do was donate a thousand dollars, would you do it?"

Maya mulled over the question. A thousand was a lot, but she would manage, she could survive it and was lucky enough to be able to bounce back from it.

"Yeah, I would."

"Well, that's the equivalent for me. I'm not a hero, Maya, I'm just doing what any caring person would do in my situation." She nodded to herself and Maya didn't have the heart to tell her that most people with her kind of wealth were nowhere near as rich in the morals department as she was.

She waited patiently while Elena dictated a quick text to Margaret saying she had resolved the situation and obtained the funding from another source.

When she looked up the clouds had cleared, and though she looked tired she seemed happy. Her smile fell slightly as she studied Maya's face.

"Are you feeling all right, sweetheart?"

Elena clearly sensed her unease and she shrugged.

"Maya, you're prepared. Ruby is ready and she's confident, things look as good as they could. I understand you're worried, and I know you miss her terribly, but please try not to stress yourself out too much."

She nodded, tears pricking the back of her eyes. She did miss Livvie, horribly. The visits every other weekend had always been hard on her. Having not seen her for almost six weeks now, she was heartbroken. Her heart tugged and pulled, straining toward her little girl, the piece of her she knew was out there somewhere, and she ached to have her back, have her home, for good.

She hadn't noticed Elena moving around her desk, but when she was pulled to her feet she went willingly into her arms, her head resting on her shoulder, slim jerking arms holding her close.

"Is there anything I can do?" Elena's voice was soft. "Do you need to go home?" She shook her head, reaching up to scrub at her eyes roughly, still held against Elena's chest.

They needed her—the benefit was so close, and they had so much to do—and she knew if she went home, she would only stew and work herself into a state worse than the one she was in now.

"I'm okay. I'm just ready for it to be over, I miss her so much."

"I know you do. I miss her too. You deserve peace, darling. Just hold on a little while longer?"

Elena made what seemed impossible sound easy, but she nodded anyway, knowing that no matter what, the time would pass, and Thursday would come. What she didn't say, unwilling to even speak it, was how terrified she was that they would lose, that she would stand before a judge, and who knew who else, all assembled to judge her, and she would be found unfit, unworthy, and she would lose Livvie for good. As it stood, she had no legal rights to visitation, it was all at Holt's discretion, and a decision against her would leave her completely at his mercy once again.

"You're hyperventilating, Maya."

Elena's voice was soft, and it brought her back. Stepping out of Elena's hold, she pressed her fingers into her eyes hard.

"Tell me how to help you."

Opening her eyes and blinking away the black spots that danced across her vision, Maya tried to steel herself. Just another forty-eight hours. She could make it; she had made it this far.

"Just...keep me busy?"

"That I can do." Elena's smile had a dark edge, and she let it drag her under, pull her away, tug her back from the rawness of her fear into something safer, more known.

*

Almost four years ago, she had stood in a similar room on the other side of the city, fresh out of prison with little more than the clothes on her back and the rapidly dwindling inheritance she had received from her parents' death. Almost four years ago, she had been found to be unfit to care for Livvie, and she had lost her.

Maya hadn't thought anything could come close to being as bad as that day. Not being arrested, not learning Neal was dead, not giving birth to her baby while handcuffed to a hospital bed and being watched by a male guard; perhaps the death of her parents did come close, but so did today.

She had forgotten, or perhaps her mind had hidden the memory. Either way, she forgot how invasive the process was: the questions, the eyes on her. Her whole sordid life history, her story, was told only in segments chosen by others, its real journey barely translating through the fractured pieces they decided selectively to drag into the light.

Ruby was a fortress at her back, strong and stable, steady and unmoved by the storm whipping around her, stinging her face and leaving her dizzy. The woman was sharp as a knife, charismatic, and built an easy rapport with the judge that Maya prayed would be enough to save her.

Her mouth moved and the right words came out. Her voice shook at first, but by the end it was strong and clear, and she delivered her responses with conviction, but inside she was still convinced it wasn't enough.

Robert was unreadable across the room from her, Bella clutching his hand, her once swollen stomach smaller now, their new baby presumably at home with the nanny. Maya knew from experience that Livvie was in the building somewhere, being kept busy by a child advocate or whatever they called them these days, some outside adult responsible for ensuring her best interests were met—as if that wasn't what the adults in the court were fighting for.

She was a long way from the scared nineteen-year-old who had once stood in her spot, brave enough now to hold the judge's eye, to return Robert's serpentine smile, and with enough years of working for this and wanting this and building for it, that when she was allowed to speak, she had a whole world to say, a million things she wanted to offer and share with the daughter she had never deserved to lose to start with.

Like driftwood she had floated through the hearing, over the waves and through the dark waters, buffeted and tossed around by questions and more.

Her fingers gripped the edge of the bench, knuckles white as she breathed and answered and tried not to think of the decision that was being made with every second.

It was finally time, it was finally almost over, and Maya felt sick under the weight of it, ready to know and eager to prolong the moment forever, because the potential outcome terrified her so much.

"Breathe, sweetheart, just breathe."

Elena leaned forward from her seat behind her, and Maya forced herself to do as she had said.

"We're in a good position, Maya. Just hang in there a little bit longer for me."

Ruby squeezed her hand and then moved to the front of the room to talk to an official looking woman who Maya had seen watching and typing frantically throughout the day.

She counted her breaths, watched the second hand move on the big official looking clock, the same government issue they had in prison, fighting her anxiety and fighting to continue to breathe, every time her thoughts strayed down an unsafe path that threatened to leave her undone.

Ruby plopped back down beside her.

"Scribe says the judge is on her way back out now."

Maya nodded, unable to feel her hands. She turned to tell Elena as much, her eyes only having time to meet Elena's before quiet fell over the room and Ruby was poking her in the ribs and telling her to stand up.

Her leaden legs were slow to react as she fought her way to her feet, her shallow breaths loud in her ears.

She was shaking as the judge recapped the hearing, and by the time she was approaching what Maya knew would be the delivering of the verdict, there were hot tears pouring down her cheeks. Elena's hand was on her waist, Ruby was squeezing her arm, and between them, they were holding her together, keeping her from being lost to the memory of last time, and the fear for this one.

She heard the words, heard that she had won, yet somehow, they didn't register. Wild-eyed, she turned to Ruby who was pulling her into a hug, congratulating her, and then Elena's arms were around her and Maya was crying.

"You did it, you did it." They pulled apart and Elena's hands were firm on her face, holding her chin up so she was looking into those familiar eyes.

"Maya, you did it."

People around them were moving, Holt's lawyer was shaking hands with Ruby, and the steward was already trying to usher them out of the room, the next party waiting to come in and start their own proceedings. Elena held her steady, her anchor in the storm, giving her a pause, a moment, a few precious seconds for reality to set in, for her to take a breath and realize she'd won.

"We got her?"

Elena's eyes were glassy, her voice soft against the noise in the room, yet somehow it was the loudest thing in Maya's head.

"Yes."

Chapter Sixteen

It was a rainy November night outside the tall ornate windows of the hall, but inside the atmosphere was warm, the winter benefit progressing well. Maya was still walking on water from the previous day. The realization that tomorrow she would pick up her daughter from Robert for good was still crashing pleasantly around her, making her smile wider, her eyes brighter, her laugh more genuine, as she moved around the room.

Elena was at her side, one hand unapologetically laced with Maya's, her dark eyes tired but shining. Donations were being made, awareness was being raised, and thus far the evening had been a roaring success, though Maya sensed something still uneasy in her girlfriend. Her smile was perfect, and she was obviously genuinely happy with the progress of the event. The people they were meeting were all supportive, and the updates throughout the night proved that the giving had been generous, yet somehow something was off with Elena.

They finally parted from an older couple they had been entertaining, and she took the opportunity to pull her aside. Snagging two champagne flutes from a passing server, she took a long sip from one before she placed it in Elena's hand, the level low enough now that her tremor wouldn't cause it to spill.

"Are you having fun, babe?"

Elena gave her a blinding smile, beautiful, all white teeth and crimson-red lipstick, and Maya knew it was designed to dazzle her, to deflect from what she was becoming increasingly aware must be an underlying problem. It almost worked. She was gorgeous in her black evening dress, smooth tan skin and silky ebony curls and two glittering diamond earrings, but Maya couldn't ignore the unease in her eyes.

"Of course. Are you?"

Maya nodded, studying her evasive gaze. Something was unsettled there, something she was trying very hard to keep from her. They had worked so hard for the benefit and on the whole they were having a good time. She smiled up at Elena, deciding to leave it alone for tonight. Elena would talk to her when she was ready, and as Winling interrupted them she realized now wasn't the best time to get into something lengthy anyway.

"Love the dress, May. Looks like a loaner from a certain lady I know who has awfully good taste."

Alicia giggled by their side, and Maya rolled her eyes, half amused, half nauseated at her friend's cheesy attempts at flattery.

"Thanks again, Alicia, for the dress. They're right, your wardrobe is really gorgeous."

Alicia shrugged.

"Keep it. It looks way better on you!"

Maya was about to interject and try to steer the conversation back to the introduction that was dying to happen but Winling beat her to it, their dark eyes full of warmth as they landed on Elena.

"Hey, Elena, I know I'm supposed to introduce myself and be all pleased to meet you, but I honestly feel like I know you already! I cannot believe she took this long to introduce us."

Elena was laughing, and Maya shoved Winling playfully, her best friend straightening their tux and dusting off the material in a totally over the top and comical display of mock offense.

"Winling, Alicia, this is Elena, my girlfriend, and the amazing woman who made all of this happen tonight."

Elena stuck out a shaking hand. Alicia was the first to bypass it and launch into her for a hug, Winling coming close behind. The acceptance, the meshing of two important parts of her world, made Maya's heart warm in a way she hadn't expected, another little piece of the impossible puzzle of her life slotting unexpectedly into place.

"It's so good to meet you, Winling, Alicia, and I can't say I'm solely responsible tonight. My employees did work very hard too."

There was a touch of something dark in her voice, and Maya met her gaze as the other two watched the interaction, the worry over her not seeming herself momentarily forgotten.

"Wow, yep... Well, you two are exactly as intense as I figured. Love the eye-fucking, kudos for that."

Maya rolled her eyes at Winling's teasing and Elena took a step closer to her.

"Oh, there's going to be much more than eye-fucking before the night is through."

Winling choked on a huge mouthful of champagne and Maya cackled at the reaction, seeing the start of a beautiful friendship between her girlfriend and her best friend.

Alicia patted them on the back sympathetically.

"Well, we'll let you ladies get back to your night. Elena, I love the dress. You have to tell me who your shopper is. We'll exchange numbers later."

Winling made a face, and Maya was glad she wasn't the only one who was on the outside of that world of personal shoppers and fancy outfits. Where it once may have made her insecure, now she just rolled her eyes along with her friend and they shared a silent moment of twin smirks at their significant others.

"Maya, let's set up an evening to go eat, okay. A double date, soon!"

Alicia's blue eyes were shining with excitement and Elena seemed equally interested.

"We should take them to Bruno's."

Alicia agreed, and Maya promised to set up the date soon, before she watched the couple drift away, grateful that they seemed to get on so well with Elena, despite her being almost fifteen years their senior too.

"Now it's my turn to ask you what you're thinking about, Miss Scott."

Ridiculously, the use of her last name still gave her chills whenever Elena said it.

"Maya..."

Robert's voice saw the high dying before it began, and she turned to meet his dark gaze, dread pooling in her stomach on a reflex.

"Robert." Elena stepped up beside her, a hand firm in hers, though this time Maya didn't baulk. Finally, she could face him herself, so far from the easily intimidated, unsure teenager she was when they had first met.

The silence was long and tense, and it was Bella who broke it.

"Livvie is so excited, she's all packed. We're going to miss her so much."

Bella had tears in her eyes, and Maya felt the sharp prick of them in her own. She cleared her throat.

"Thank you so much for everything you did for her... both of you."

Bella nodded, dabbing at her eyes, and even Robert looked a little choked up.

"Congratulations on your family, Miss Scott." He looked between her and Elena. "You've built a life for yourself that you ought to be proud of. We'll miss Livvie very much, but I trust she's in good hands."

The words stunned her, and she noticed how old Robert looked, how he leaned heavier on his cane than he once had, the gray almost totally covering his once black head of hair.

They turned to leave, and she caught his hand.

"It doesn't have to be all or nothing." She blurted the words, heat rushing to her cheeks when Robert turned back to look at her. "You're Livvie's grandfather and she loves you and Bella, so much. There will always be a place in her life for you both if you want it."

Bella was nodding frantically, and Robert swallowed hard.

"We'd like that, Maya."

She offered him a tentative smile, the tide between them shifting, something new, something better, growing from the change.

"Let's meet up next week. Maybe you two can come over and eat with us, and we'll work everything out, so you still get to spend time with her?"

Elena squeezed her hand intentionally and a weight lifted from her chest. She knew she had done the right thing.

"Let me know if you need us to bring anything." Bella rushed forward and hugged her, and Maya held her tight, a strange sense of family creeping over her.

"Please, enjoy the evening, we'll see you next week?"

Elena hugged Bella, too, and shook Robert's hand, closing the interaction as they disappeared into the crowded space and she turned back to her.

"I'm so proud of you, Maya."

Before she could reply, there was a buzz over the sound system and Margaret's soft voice was cutting through the chatter asking for their attention from the stage.

"Good evening, everyone. My name is Margaret Bouchere, I'm the managing director of the Mars Fund. Thank you all for coming tonight to support our benefit. The funds raised this evening will be instrumental in supporting not one, not two, but *fifteen* children's charities across the country as they assist the young people who need it!"

A cheer broke out and Maya clapped along with the audience.

"By the end of the night, we hope your stomachs and hearts are full, and your wallets are empty!"

Everyone laughed.

"I'm up here on stage because we felt someone on our team deserves special recognition for her outstanding contribution to the evening."

Anticipation hung over the room for a few seconds.

"Elena, where are you?"

Maya stepped sideways, waving to Margaret, people turning one by one in their direction, to locate the woman being summoned. Elena gave an embarrassed half wave up at the stage.

"Right. Elena Mars, ladies and gents, our CEO, the creator of this event and its largest contributor and champion. In order to make tonight a reality, Elena donated over twenty-five thousand dollars of her own personal money."

The crowd went wild.

"In addition to this, she has worked tirelessly all year to make the evening a success. Enough so that I'm hoping she's going to be too tired to kill me for embarrassing her like this."

Maya squeezed Elena's hand tight in her own, immensely proud, and grateful to Margaret for her kind words that were so well deserved.

"So, with all that said, Elena, would you like to come up here and say a few words of your own?"

Maya walked with her, the crowd talking in low voices as they made their way steadily to the front. When they reached the stairs Maya walked her up, surprised when Elena turned and kissed her on the lips.

"Wait here for me?"

She nodded, feeling the blush on her cheeks from the public display of affection, sure beyond doubt she was the envy of many men and women in the audience at that moment.

Elena took the mic, and she was radiant. For the first time all evening she seemed to settle, and Maya watched her, spellbound, still marveling at her luck that such an amazing woman somehow chose to be with her.

"Good evening."

Her voice shook a little, her head jerking to the side before she corrected it, hands clutching the mic stand to keep them steady in place.

"Before we go any further, in light of Margaret's kind words, I would also like to take the opportunity to thank everyone at The Mars Foundation. This evening, and all our projects this year have been very much team efforts, and none of it would be possible without them."

The room applauded, and Elena slapped her open palms against her thighs. Maya knew this was her way of joining the applause, the actual motion of clapping her hands repeatedly being incredibly difficult for her to coordinate.

"Our evening is far from over. We still have the silent auction to look forward to, as well as the results from the raffle. To echo Margaret's sentiments, I hope you will all continue to give generously to these most worthy causes, and take the time to read the information cards on your table and get to know a few of our charities who will benefit directly, and completely, from all proceeds raised tonight."

She took a breath. Maya watched her tongue dart out to wet her lips, and as she glanced sideways to catch her eyes there was a nervousness there that Maya couldn't place.

"Before we return to our celebrations, I have one more thing I would like to say. This has been a banner year for TMF, with over half a million dollars raised and counting, but also, it's been an important year for me too. For many years I've struggled to talk about—hell, to even *acknowledge* my disability for fear of how it might disadvantage me in my ability to do my job and live my life."

The room was silent. Those who knew Elena were clearly staggered by her words, and those who didn't seemed to feel the seriousness of the moment.

"Tonight, I'm proud to stand before you all as a disabled woman with cerebral palsy and announce the unveiling of a final recipient charity for this Benefit. The CPKC, also known as Cerebral Palsy Kids Can, a charity out of Ocala, Florida that supports children living with CP."

Everyone was clapping, and Maya clapped along with them, pausing to swipe a stray tear from her cheek.

"I spent a large part of my adult life terrified of not being accepted by the world because of my CP, and in doing this, I also succeeded in not fully accepting myself. Some of you already know I met a wonderful woman this year by the name of Maya Scott."

Heat exploded on Maya's cheeks, yet she was still able to hold her head up as all eyes in the room turned to her, though she cared only about the familiar brown ones that were on her, a soft smile on Elena's face.

"As well as doing wonderful things as an employee at TMF, she also worked her magic on me personally."

Elena swallowed hard, and time slowed down until Maya could hear the thudding of her own heart over the words amplified through the mic.

"Somewhere between falling in love with her, and a little girl who is a more ruthless dealmaker than half the executives I deal with on a daily basis—" She was interrupted by laughter. "I also learned to fall in love with myself, my whole self, disability and all. And it was because of your love, Maya, your support, your bull-headed stubborn refusal to deal with my crap, that I stand where I stand today, the happiest I have been my entire life."

She took a deep breath, and Maya struggled to breathe.

"Could you come here, darling?"

The walk across the stage was ethereal, and Maya was floating, watching herself from above, watching as Margaret appeared by Elena's side. She pressed something into her hand with a teary smile and held her elbow as she struggled down to one knee, ended up instead on two, and then sat on her bottom on the stage when she lost her balance totally.

The crowd laughed, cheered, applauded, and Maya was crying, hot tears of joy and love and disbelief because this didn't happen to her, this kind of fairytale was just not her life.

Still sitting on the floor, Elena opened the box to see a beautiful opalescent diamond shining under the stage lights.

"Maya, you showed me a life I thought I could never be lucky enough to have, a love I never dreamed I could deserve, and I probably still don't. But if it's all right with you, I would very much like to keep trying to deserve you, for a very long time. Will you marry me?"

She heard Winling hooting somewhere in the crowd as she nodded, glad to hit the floor on shaking knees and kiss the woman of her dreams, the one who by some dream or magic or complete and utter miracle loved her enough to want to keep her, forever.

Epilogue

They were sitting around a set of teacups, a fire roaring in Elena's wood burner warding off the chill outside.

"So, you marry My'lena, Mama, and My'lena marry you?"

Maya nodded, forcing herself not to bite her lip, not to let any of her nerves show on her face. Livvie had taken everything so well so far as they explained their relationship to her.

Elena's dark eyes were on the teacups, and Maya could sense her nervousness too. Elena had hardly slept the previous night and had woken her up twice to insist they didn't have to tell the girl once, and then worry about confusing her or upsetting her the other time. Maya knew that beneath her concern for Livvie, Elena was also terrified of being rejected.

An advocate had met with them, along with Bella and Robert earlier in the month while they helped Livvie to understand that she would be living with Maya and Elena at the mansion from now on, but would still get to see Grandpa and Bella. The little girl's resilience and openness through the change amazed Maya. Although she had taken everything in stride, particularly her huge new bedroom at the mansion which Elena had let her pick out an obnoxious bright-purple paint for, she constantly worried that her daughter wasn't really adapting as well as they all thought.

For her part, Elena had taken to parenting like she had done it all her life, her office hours rearranged effortlessly so she could take Livvie to the best pre-k in the city. Somehow around her busy work schedule, she still found time to cook for them, to make lunches, for stories and tea parties, and Maya was in awe of her. Her decision to get Livvie back had been completely validated by the wonderful life she had been able to give her, now that Elena was a part of it.

A little hand reached out and touched the stone on her engagement ring, the other hand poking Elena in the ribs periodically from her position on her lap.

They were beautiful together, Elena's tan skin and warm loving eyes smiling down on the fair-haired little girl who absolutely adored her. Once again, Maya's life felt far too much like a fairytale to be real, and now she seemed set to spend it with the two of them, she wondered if that feeling would ever stop.

"Bella say some people has a mommy and a mommy." Livvie leaned toward her like she was telling Maya something profound. "And her says some people can have a daddy and a daddy. I not have any daddies."

Maya's heart sunk.

"But you and My'lena, Mama."

She lost track a bit at that and waited for the babbling to continue. Instead, Livvie looked up at Elena, her words suddenly growing careful as she puzzled through the situation aloud.

"So, if my mama and then you. You be my mommy but my mama?"

Maya stopped breathing, instantly grasping the shy question, as she watched Elena replay the words again. She was just about to open her mouth to try to clarify when Elena spoke.

"I love you, and I love Mama and if it's all right with you I would really like to be your mommy too." Elena swallowed thickly. "Do you think that would be okay?"

Maya's heart melted but she still held her breath, knowing her daughter's unpredictability could make this answer something wonderful or something terrible, or something downright weird.

A tear spilled down Elena's cheek and Livvie giggled, swatting it away before it could fall on her. Her big green eyes shone as she looked up Elena.

"Okay, Mommy."

About the Author

L.E. Royal is a British born fiction writer, living in Texas. She enjoys dark but redeemable characters and twisted themes. Though she is a fan of happy endings, she would describe most of her work as fractured romance. When she is not writing, she is pursuing her dreams with her champion Arabian show horses or hanging out at her small ranch/accidental cat sanctuary.

Email: L.E.Royal@outlook.com

Facebook: www.facebook.com/le.royal.writes

Twitter: @leroyalwrites

Website: www.leroyalauthor.com/home

Other NineStar books by this author

Blood Echo

Blood Lust

Never Knew Until You

Also Available from NineStar Press

Connect with NineStar Press

www.ninestarpress.com

www.facebook.com/ninestarpress

www.facebook.com/groups/NineStarNiche

www.twitter.com/ninestarpress

Printed in Great Britain
by Amazon